family

matthew costello

13Thirty Books
Print and Digital Editions
Copyright 2017

Discover new and exciting works by Matthew Costello and 13Thirty Books at www.13thirtybooks.com

ISBN: 0-9977912-5-X
ISBN-13: 978-0-9977912-5-9

DEDICATION

To my wife, Ann, my kids, Devon, Nora, Chris… my *family* that taught me what is really important in life.

ACKNOWLEDGMENTS

A special thanks to Brendan Deneen, editor extraordinaire, who decades ago became fascinated with a short story called 'Vacation', and one day would convince its author to turn it into a novel – and a series.

one

Into the E.R.

1
Central New Jersey

Montvale Memorial Hospital
1:10 a.m.

Christie looked over at her daughter Kate, at her hands gripped so tightly on the steering wheel, head leaning forward as if that might help her drive... help her navigate.

They had just stopped at the gate that barred the way to the hospital parking lot, with the entrance to the ER visible at one corner of the building.

Her first thought, *No guards.*

And then, *The gate isn't opening.*

C'mon, she thought.

Christie looked down at her leg, her jeans jacket serving as a tourniquet, now soaked through, doing little to stem the blood.

She looked back at Kate.

Not even old enough to have a learner's permit.

And yet, here she was, having driven them from the madness at the Mountain Inn.

Madness.

When people—normal people, not monsters like the cannibals, the twisted humans that came to be called "Can Heads"—showed up in the middle of the night and began rounding up people.

Especially the young.

God. For food.

Because Kate had seen what their plans were for the young.

"Blast the horn, Kate."

Kate hit the horn once, then again.

Still, the gate didn't move.

"Mom, maybe the hospital isn't open. Maybe it just looks open. Maybe we need go someplace else..."

Christie could hear the fear in Kate's voice—and not just the fear of what was out in the darkness that surrounded them.

No, her daughter could look down in the dim interior light of the car and see how sodden and dark the jacket wound around Christie's right leg had become.

Simon, in the back, had said nothing.

Even when Christie had looked back at her son, when she had turned to ask, "*You okay, Simon?*"

Just a nod.

The boy's face locked, set in a way that Christie wasn't sure she had ever seen before, despite everything they had all been through.

As soon as possible she'd have to really talk to him, talk to them both. About what happened.

Christie reminding herself: *I'm still the parent.*

Another loud beep from Kate, and then—over the rumble of their car—Christie heard the slow clanking of the gate mechanism kicking in, the chain-link gate beginning to slid open.

Again, the disturbing thought.

How come there are no guards out here, no people with guns?

No one keeping watch over this place, this hospital that is supposedly open?

And that thought turned even more disturbing with each *clickety-clack* of the electric gate sliding to its fully open position.

Is it electrified?

Had to be, she thought. *These days, had to be.*

She was sure if she looked around she'd spot one of those friendly warning signs, with big block letters announcing:

WARNING! THIS GATE IS ELECTRIFIED! IF YOU TOUCH
IT YOU WILL DIE!

Did anyone have a gate or fence today, in this world, that *wasn't*
electrified?

The gate now open, she touched Kate's left shoulder.

"Go on, Kate. Nice and slowly. Find a spot to park."

And showing Kate's newness with the accelerator, the car
lurched forward, once, then again. But despite the jerky moves, the
car rolled inside the hospital compound, and looking back quickly,
Christie watched the gate close.

Nothing slipping in behind them.

That was the important thing to check.

Always look behind.

She turned back to the parking spaces.

"Over *there*. Near the Emergency Room door."

Still no one around, no one coming out so see who had just
driven into the compound.

And Kate made the car lurch forward a few feet, then braked in
reaction, slowly trying to slide into a parking space.

None of this is easy for her.

"You're going good, Kate. Just a little closer..."

And meanwhile, Christie kept looking around.

It didn't feel right.

So quiet.

Then Kate stopped, the engine still running, the car parked at
an angle, the best she could do.

Christie took another look behind, past Simon, who was also
looking around.

Of course.

Or course, he'd also look around.

The gate shut, and the darkness beyond total. The area around
the hospital seemed empty.

"Okay," Christie said. "You can shut the ignition off."

Kate hesitated as if not understanding.

"Turn the key. To the left. And kill the lights."

Immediately regretting the choice of words.

No one needed to hear the word "kill" any more than necessary.

The car went silent, lights off. This old Camry, with gas, and battery in good shape, represented their ability to stay alive, Christie knew.

Without it, they were lost.

But when she saw Kate about to pull on the door handle, she said, "No. Wait a bit."

Their doors were locked.

Not a time to rush into anything. It might all be fine inside that building. But either way, better being cautious.

And anyone inside—that is, if there was anyone inside—would be watching the car carefully as well.

They had let us in.

But they would be watching carefully who came out of the car.

Especially if they knew—like she did—that things had changed.

That it just wasn't humans versus Can Heads anymore.

Something different had happened, at least in this part of the world.

There were humans; there were the animal-like Can Heads.

And then, *There were others.*

She looked back at Simon.

Those others who had captured Simon. Were ready to take him away.

She gave Simon a smile. He had been taken by them, captured until Kate fired her gun and stopped them.

She had saved her brother.

From people who were even more monstrous than Can Heads.

"Shouldn't we go in, Mom? Look at your leg!"

Christie quickly shook her head. "No. Keep the doors locked, okay…"

Their father's voice—his constant warning in all their heads— 'Doors locked, windows up, everyone."

That voice gone forever.

And in that moment, that knowledge—so hard to accept—hurt way more than the oozing wound on her right leg.

"Mom," Simon said, his voice she thought, low, hollow, "I have to pee."

Such a human thing. Though Simon was no little kid, could never be a little kid after all he had seen and done, still… the age-old words.

Mom, I've got to pee.

"Right, Simon. Just want to be sure everything's… okay here."

She knew he would understand that well enough.

Only hours before he'd had a rope tight around his neck, herded by people—seemingly normal, everyday people—into a truck.

And Christie had seen where they were taking these kids.

To that warehouse. And when those people decided to move on, they'd bring those kids with them because, because—

She cut off those thoughts.

No benefit in summoning those feelings. She didn't need anything further to be horrified about, to terrify her.

She turned back to Simon again, forcing a smile. "Just a few minutes, Simon. Okay? Just let's wait."

Then back to the bright windows.

Where the hell were the people? Was this hospital deserted, a tantalizing, brightly lit place that was in fact completely empty?

She'd have to do something soon.

Get out, go in—or leave?

But how long could she last, oozing blood? And then what would happen, with the two kids on their own?

Another thought to be quickly squelched.

Then—back to movement.

She saw a shape, shadowy, toward the back of the ER entrance. As if laying back, waiting.

And what exactly was that shape?

Somebody who worked here?

Or just another Can Head hoping that this was their lucky night.

Then again: *Can't just stay here.*

"Mom—we just going to sit here?" Kate asked. "Look at your leg!"

Christie was all too aware of her leg. The pain excruciating, the throbbing constant, a slippery pool forming at her feet from the dripping blood.

"Right." She looked at Kate, forced a smile. "We can't just sit here."

Kate nodded, her hands still locked on the steering wheel.

And like pulling the lever on something deadly, Christie grabbed her door handle and just held it, about to be opened to the unknown.

She took a breath.

2
Is Anybody In There?

It had only been minutes, but it seemed an eternity.

"Okay, kids. Here's what we'll do. When I say *now*, we get out and make our way over there, and—"

"Mom, can you even walk?"

Christie didn't know the answer to that question. Walk? Earlier she had barely made it to the car, leaning on Kate.

Could she even do that now? Was that even possible?

"I think so, Kate. I may need…"

No. Better be honest.

"I will need your help. Right—so, Kate, you circle around, and help me out. And Simon…"

Another look back.

"You get out and go to the hospital door, but don't go in. Not till Kate and I are there."

A nod. Then a question.

"Can I have my gun?"

Like asking for an allowance.

And this grim question was now Christie's to answer. "Yes. Pointed down, safety on. Everything your father showed you."

Back to Kate who—Christie knew, with her leg wound—was the real adult here.

Still a kid, a teenager, and yet the adult.

"Ready, Kate?"

"Yeah, Mom."

Her daughter didn't need to ask whether she should bring her gun. Not after taking out the men who had tried to herd Simon into their van.

Kate and her gun would be inseparable.

Another change in this world that seemed to change daily.

"Okay."

A deep breath, air filling her lungs, steeling herself for just about anything.

"Now…"

And the door locks popped up, crackling like the sounds of muffled gunshots, and they all got out of the car.

*

That first bit of pressure on the wounded leg, and Christie saw brilliant flashes of light before her eyes.

Then she put her left leg down, taking as much of her weight as possible as Kate scurried around and quickly came to Christie's right side.

Simon stood just behind them.

"Ready, Mom?"

Christie nodded, not at all sure she was ready. She gave another glance at the ER entrance ahead.

Nothing.

Kate slid her arm around her mother and, using leverage more than strength, tried to help Christie up.

Just doing that was agony.

Not even a step taken, but getting horizontal made tears come to her eyes. And Christie knew that if she blacked out, there would be no way that her kids could get her into the building by themselves.

Will anyone come out to help?

Who knows?

Because it seemed like no one inside gave a damn about

whatever the hell was going on in here.

Best done quickly, she thought.

Now, with Kate's help, she began hopping on her good leg, gaining only inches with each hop. She kept her dripping, sodden leg off the ground as best she could.

But with so little strength in that leg, the tip of her right foot dragged as she hopped. Each hop making that bloody wound crease just a bit as the wound constantly moved back and forth, opening, shutting.

Excruciating pain.

Could she even make it to the entrance?

Then, with Simon right behind, she felt a tap on her shoulder.

Another hop. She didn't turn back to her son; no, they had to get to the door and fast.

"What, Simon?" She tried to keep her voice level, steady, free of the pain that had grown overwhelming.

And knowing that she completely failed in that.

Turning testy. "What is it, Simon?"

"They're there, Mom. Out there. Where we just came from. I see them."

Her heart sank.

Thinking, *What a horrible trap this could be.*

Can Heads were more like animals; devoid of reasoning, planning. But like any feral animal, these once-humans clearly could hunt and work together.

She knew that now.

And she had no choice but to pause before the next hop and look over her shoulder, to the gate where they entered.

And sure enough, they stood there.

A row of five... six Can Heads. Their clothes tattered to the point where they were mostly naked. But with just enough clothing so she could see this one was a woman, this a man, this one... bit of a dress... shorter, the size of her own Kate.

Once a young girl. Now a monster.

"Let's go," she said, more to herself than to her kids.

But she was close to telling them to make a run for it. And if she herself had to crawl to the entryway, then that is exactly what she would do.

Another look back.

Just as one Can Head, seemingly agitated by how close she and her kids were, raised its hands.

Right to the fence.

Then it grabbed at the wire-mesh fence as if ready to climb, leap over, and pounce on them.

The ER door still yards away.

But as she looked—the Can Head's hands locked on the fence—sparks flew. The creature shook and rattled, its hands still locked on the fence, until it seemed to explode backward from the electrified fence, falling to the ground where its fellow creatures ignored it.

All of them wanting *in* so badly.

But with enough of a sliver of awareness to realize that maybe grabbing the fence was a bad thing to do.

The Can Heads with the savviness of a wolf pack, like recognizing that a fire at a campsite could hurt, could be dangerous.

Christie turned back to the door.

"Almost there, Mom," Kate said, her voice so sweet, so encouraging.

My girl, Christie thought.

Then, remembering Jack, never far from her thoughts... *our girl*.

Another hop, and the pain made Christie moan.

Again, and now she could reach out and touch the glass door.

"Bang on it. Kate, Simon. Bang on the door!"

The stupid, goddamn door.

Her kids did as she asked. Simon walked over to a buzzer that read: Press For Admission After Hours.

After hours.

Wasn't it always "after hours" these days? Doors always locked.

Simon pressed again, and Christie could barely hear the high-pitched whine made by the buzzer.

Had they come here for nothing?

"Bang again, kids."

She realized her voice sounded like a sob; she had to be scaring them even more.

Last thing in the world that she wanted to do. Scare them. *They don't deserve any more of that.*

And then—from the side out of sight—she saw men, three of them, rifles held at forty-five degree angles, walk to the door. Their faces grim, eyes hooded, dark as if they had been up for hours.

Christie shook her head.

What the hell is wrong with them?

She made her voice as loud as she could.

"Let us in, please."

She turned to her two kids as if seeing that she had children with her would make these grim-faced men open the door.

And then, coming from behind them, a vision in white.

A gray-haired man pushed past them, his doctor's coat flapping open.

And while the men just stood there, the doctor hit a button to the right side of the door.

Each of the men raised their guns. Ready. Just in case.

And the door whooshed open. The warm air inside hitting Christie, the doctor looking over the three of them as if expecting them to simply cross the threshold themselves.

Until he turned to the men and said, his voice biting, tired, sounding so stressed.

"Help them in, damn it."

And finally, one man came to Christie's left, another to her right, relieving Kate. A third man quickly ushered the kids in, his lead pivoting left and right, and again… left and right, and he nearly pushed the kids into the ER.

And once there, the doctor hit a button and the door quickly shut behind them.

Which is when Christie—and she didn't know the reason, *Why now?*—began crying as a tall man with a long rifle held her up.

3
A Stitch in Time

As the men guided Christie down a corridor, she looked to the right.

At nearly every window someone squatted with a gun, head low, staring out into the chilly night.

No one patrolling outside, she thought.

Made sense. Better to use the hospital itself as a fort.

Many of the windows had holes that had been taped up with cardboard and duct tape.

Signs of previous incursions.

Does their power ever fail here?

On those powerless nights do the Can Heads come crawling over the top of that fence?

She looked back. Kate and Simon followed her, alone now, trailing the two men and the doctor, who moved Christie through the ER corridor as fast as they could.

Until they reached a room.

"In here," the doctor said. "Come on."

His voice tired, maybe defeated.

What has he seen these weeks? The wounded, the dead? And this could very well be the only operating facility for miles around.

The men brought Christie beside a hospital bed.

"Okay," one said. "Ready?"

And they lifted her up, tilting her, and slowly slid her onto the bed.

Which is when the doctor turned to her two kids, their eyes locked on her.

They have to be so worried, she thought.

So terribly scared.

"Um, kids," the doctor said. "Can you wait outside? Down the hall. There's chairs."

For a moment, they didn't move.

They had become people who no longer automatically did what someone told them.

But Christie didn't know what was ahead... what would happen in this room.

"Kate... Simon... best you wait. I'll be fine."

The word sounding ridiculous.

Fine.

She looked right at her daughter. "Kate. Please."

And then, another heart-breaking moment among so many on this night of nights, she saw Kate take Simon's hand.

"Come on," she said simply.

Simon nodded, didn't shake off her hand, his face still looking so set; whatever thoughts he had, his worries, all unvoiced, hidden.

And he let Kate lead him away.

The men stood there for a moment. "Anything else, Doc?" one said.

"Try to get Karen to come in. For a bit, at least."

The men nodded, and left.

And only then did the doctor, his snow-white hair in disarray as if he had touched something loaded with static electricity, come close to her.

"Let's see... what we have going on here." Then, for the first time, a bit of a smile. "Your name?"

"Christie. Christie Murphy. I-I—"

But the doctor nodded. No need for more information. No

need for insurance cards. No forms to be filled out.

Just someone else who had been attacked by the plague of humans that everyone called Can Heads. People turned into animals. People who ate their own kind.

And then there was this thought: Can we even call them people anymore?

She saw a nametag on his white jacket.

Dr. Martin.

Like that British TV show she liked. The English village, the quirky doctor.

The doctor reached for the sodden jeans jacket, now such a deep crimson, and with every movement, every touch, causing such intense pain, he began unwrapping it.

*

She wondered why the doctor didn't give her a painkiller.

They have to have painkillers, she thought. *No way they could be out of them*. Because if they were, God—then this was going to be worse than anything she could imagine.

But the doctor, who had been quiet during the unwrapping process—leaning close, his wireframes filmy, days away from their last cleaning—looked close at the wound and nodded.

"I'll give you something in a bit," he said. "I needed to see where you have the most pain. With what we have here, it helps." A small smile. "Not scientific, but it could tell me whether we have major nerve damage as well as muscle tears, blood loss."

"And?" Christie said, her eyes still watery from the pain.

"I think… think, *no*. Nothing major. You've lost a lot of blood. Something we don't have a lot of. Your blood type?"

"O positive."

A nod, neither confirming nor denying the possibility that this place had stores of that type of plasma.

"I can stitch up parts of the wound, and bandage the rest. Tell you. It won't be pretty. And there may be some mobility issues afterwards. But I'm afraid it's all we can do here. Can't do any tissue transplants, and besides—"

"That will be fine."

He stopped, and looked at her, eyes making contact.

"You need to do what will get me up and with my kids the fastest."

Dr. Martin took a breath.

Not at all like the fussy Cornwall physician on TV, in his pressed suit.

"We can talk about that later. But I best get going."

At that moment, a woman came in, burly, hair in a bun, in a white nurse's uniform that Christie could see was dotted with stains.

She didn't even look at Christie as she hurried in.

But the doctor turned to her. "Karen, I'm going to do some stitching, then I'll need a large trauma bandage for the rest of the wound. Can we also get some type O plasma going, and—"

Now back to Christie.

"Going to knock you out now, Christie. This will take a while. Will be morning when you wake up. Hopefully"—the smallest of smiles—"all done."

Christie nodded, as Karen walked over to a wall, and wheeled an instrument tray close to the bed.

Not till morning.

Would Kate… Simon… be all right?

"Can you explain to my kids? They'll worry."

A nod.

The nurse brought over some vials to the tray.

"Morphine," the doctor said, quickly filling a syringe. "Should do the trick while we get the blood going, stop the pain. We'll get a patch on you as well for when you come to."

He stuck the needle in one end of the small container, and then, bringing the syringe close for inspection, leaned close to Christie.

"In the hip, on your good side, will be best. I'll also inject the wound area with a powerful local aesthetic. Just in case."

But Christie had a question.

"Doctor... you must have seen people. Like me. Attacked, bloody."

"Yes. Lately... so many. Like it's getting worse."

"So, a question."

The physician waited.

"Is it ever like... a contagion? Something that happens to people when they're bitten." She took a breath. "Are people the same afterward."

The doctor again looked her straight in the eyes.

"I don't pretend to know much about this... thing. These Can Heads. How—I mean—how did it all happen? Has anyone told us?"

She heard frustration, even rage, in his voice.

A man of science reduced to dealing with the victims of human monsters, with no one knowing where they came from.

The doctor stopped.

Another breath. Christie wondered: Is he the only doctor still left here? Does this whole hospital, all its patients, land on his shoulders?

Then this...

How long could they hold out here? When will the gates fail and the place be overwhelmed?

Not a matter of *if*, Christie thought.

But *when*.

"I'll tell you what I've seen. Bites, flesh ripped out, a lot worse than this. And afterwards—those who lived at least—they seemed the same. So I say... no, this isn't like rabies. Not like TV... those grisly movies. No, when people die from a Can Head attack, they stay dead. And when they survive, they seem... fine."

He brought the needle close.

"Shall we start?"

Christie nodded, the doctor's words reassuring.

And yet she had to wonder.

Fine.

Physically. But inside people's heads, when they sleep at night, when they *try* to sleep at night.

Could they ever be the same?

The needle pricked her skin in her left hip.

"Just will take seconds," the doctor said. "Everything should start fading in a minute."

That seemed impossible. That this night, the attack at the Mountain Inn, their escape, sweet Kate driving. How could that fade with just a slim needle sliding into her hip?

Until... it did.

4

Morning

As soon as Christie opened her eyes, she felt the pain.

But what last night had been a spike-like feeling spearing her thigh now felt dull and throbbing.

Sun poured through the windows, the blinds open so the hospital room filled with light.

She licked her lips, dry and cracked, feeling so thirsty. She turned to the end table beside the hospital bed and saw a plastic cup with a lid. A straw stuck from the top.

Had someone given her water during the night?

She had no memory of the night, of sipping water, of anything except that moment she felt the pin-prick of the syringe entering her left side.

Her "good side" as the doctor called it. In moments, all was blackness.

Now she still felt woozy, as if she had been partying with one drink too many.

But so thirsty…

She reached awkwardly with her left hand, her arm moving like a badly working crane stretching to the cup. Fingers closed on it, and she brought it close to her mouth, making a few attempts before her lips finally landed on the straw end and she could suck in the precious liquid.

Tepid—but still so amazingly delicious when it hit her dry mouth.

Which is when the nurse came in.

Had she been up all night? Was she the only nurse?

Christie tried to recall her name, drawing a blank for a second. Then it came: *Karen.*

"Ah, you're up. I'll let the doctor know."

The woman moved efficiently through the room, lowering the blinds so the sun didn't make everything glow so brilliantly. Then, grabbing a clipboard and a look up to the monitors, to the IV drip.

"All looking good, sweetie. How's the pain?" Then, before an answer, "Let me get you some ice water."

Christie nodded.

Ice. Cold, cold ice . . .

She took the cup from Christie's lips and dumped what was in it into a sink across from the bed.

"How's the pain, Christie?"

Pain.

"Um, not like it was. Can feel the bandage."

"And you got some stitches as well. Looked pretty good when he was done. Think the wound seemed worse than it was, all so bloody. Once we had it cleaned up, not so bad."

Karen came to the bed, and pushing aside Christie's hospital gown near her right shoulder, exposed a two-inch white square.

"Right. Your morphine patch. He'll want you on lighter stuff. Thinking . . . you might mend fast. That will be good?"

Christie nodded. Last night, she hadn't had any thoughts other than getting to the hospital, getting help.

Now talk of "mending fast." The wound not so bad.

Christie turned right, to her IV drip. No blood hanging up there; they must have given her some, and that was done.

Karen reached down and grabbed Christie's wrist as if she was a doll, lifeless, at the whim of this bustling woman who you might look at and think, *well, she must have gotten a solid eight hours of sleep.*

So alert.

Cheery even!

The nurse looked at a large clock on the wall facing the bed.

"Pulse good." A smile, as her eyes went from the clock to Christie. "Everything looking good. Maybe even a bit to eat later. Some lunch?"

Eating.

When was the last time she had actually eaten something? But however long it had been, there was no rumble in her stomach signaling that she was hungry.

Christie took a breath.

She had a question and it would take an effort asking them.

"It all went well?"

Karen nodded, smiled reassuringly. "Perfectly. But you can talk to the doctor about that. Any questions you have."

Maybe not so perfectly, she thought.

But then a different kind of question.

"My kids…"

Karen nodded. "Right. We found a room for them, got them some food, told them you would be fine. Nice kids. Been through something? All of you."

Karen's smile faded as she asked the question.

Been through something.

Guess you could say that.

"They slept okay. I checked on them in a bit. Worried about you, of course. Real good kids you got there."

Christie nodded. "Can I see them?"

After last night—after what she had seen—the idea of not knowing where her kids where, not having them close by, immediately put a pit in her stomach.

Though this nurse seemed so helpful, warm, *efficient*, trust was something that had faded in Christie's universe.

She struggled to raise her head a bit. To make her request seem less like begging, more forceful.

To make it absolutely clear.

"I want to see them."

The nurse's eyes narrowed. "Usually, we like you to be up a bit, get your head clear, you know. As I said, they're fine, and—"

"I want to see them now."

The voice steady. Not snapping at the woman. But repeating what she wanted.

Karen stopped, nodded.

"Okay. Let me just check with the doctor, and I'll go get them. Sure you're able to… talk? Probably still a bit wobbly."

Christie nodded, not really knowing whether she was in any shape to talk to them.

But no. It wasn't as if she had things to be discussed. No plans forming at all. For now, it was enough that they walked in here, and she could touch their hands, give them a smile, to let them know it was all okay.

Finally, Christie said: "I'm all right. Thank you."

"All righty then. Be a few. Like I said, gotta check with the doctor. He's usually *numero uno* to see a recovering patient." The woman paused, leaned close. "But I get it. And… I'll go get them."

And then she turned and left the room, crossing the zebra stripes of sun and shadow on the hospital room floor made by the morning light on this bright day.

*

Kate walked into the room so slowly, with Simon just steps behind.

Christie quickly smiled—but no smiles came back. Instead the kids kept walking toward the bed with tentative steps that seemed better suited for a funeral than a hospital visit.

She decided to try humor.

"I don't look *that* bad, do I?"

But now with both of them beside her, Christie saw that that didn't work at all.

Not a time for humor.

So we'll be serious, she thought.

And she had to wonder what the impact of all this—last night, their trip home after Jack sacrificed his life for them, the guns...

Their stay in the Mountain Inn that turned into a trap.

The guns... the killing...

What toll would it take on them?

"Mom," Kate finally said, "are you okay?"

Christie worked to keep the smile on her face. She reached out and grabbed Kate's left hand. A squeeze, then the same to Simon.

She struggled to speak in as normal a voice as she could.

"Well—I haven't spoken to the doctor this morning. But sure feels better. All bandaged. No real pain. Unless I move, that is."

Her daughter nodded.

"And you two... you were okay last night?"

She saw Kate look at Simon, the boy barely turning his head to his sister. As if there shared a secret that wasn't about to be revealed.

"We were okay. They got us some food. Mostly potatoes and peas. A room to sleep in."

Christie nodded as best she could with her head against the pillow.

Something else for her to worry about.

Her kids without her. What did they really know about this place, the people here?

Then again, these days, what did they know about anyplace?

"Good. And you both slept?"

Two nods.

"Great." Then she looked right at Kate, needing her to hear something.

"Kate, I couldn't have done this... gotten here without you. You know that, right?"

Another nod. "Wasn't so hard," Kate said. "The driving."

Finally Simon spoke. "Bet I could do it," he said—a flash of her old son, always competing with his older sister.

And Christie turned to Simon, smile broadening. She thought of how Kate had found him last night, rope tight around his neck, being led away.

Does he know—does Simon have any idea at all—where they were taking him, what they would do?

She hoped to God... not.

And then Simon, seeing their neighbor, the always upbeat, always hopeful Helen, who fired her cannon-like shotgun with the steadiness of a cowboy.

Simon seeing her killed.

In mere seconds, all those thoughts. Thoughts that she knew she had to somehow get past.

"I bet you could too, Simon. Maybe, when I'm a bit better, lessons for you."

"Mom..." Kate protested, finally a bit back to form as the older sister with her prerogatives, "he's years away from a license."

"I know," Christie said. Back to take Kate's hand with another squeeze, hoping she'd get the message.

That message...

Does any of that matter anymore?

Licenses, permits, laws?

Kate didn't say anything more.

Good girl, Christie thought.

But then Simon asked a question which—since she had come to—Christie hadn't thought about.

"Mom, what are we going to do?"

Christie let the simple question hang for a few moments.

It was a question that made Christie look away, back to the blinds slicing the sunlight into perfect strips that hit the linoleum floor.

"Right now, I don't know, Simon. I mean, I just woke up. Don't really know how my leg is. Don't know what's going on here, or the towns nearby or..."

What's happening in the whole goddamned country.

Does anybody?

"So let's take it a day at a time. The doctor is coming in soon. I'll find out as much as I can."

But Simon didn't let it go.

"I don't think we can just stay here, Mom. Staying places isn't a good idea."

Christie nodded. She knew what he meant.

If you stayed places, bad things happened.

"Simon," she said, "I know."

He had to be worried about this place, any place these days. And with their mother laid up in bed, the kids must be more scared, more alone, than they ever have been.

Then—an idea.

"I tell you this. Just for you two. No need for anyone else to know. I'll find out how I'm doing. I'll learn as much as I can about this hospital. This town, you know what I mean?"

Her two children nodded.

"And then, just the three of us—together—we'll plan. Together we'll decide what to do."

The absurdity of it—letting kids be part of what could be such a large decision—seeming not absurd at all.

Not when those kids have done what they've done.

They've had to grow up fast, like survivors trapped in any terror, any tragedy.

Grow up so fast—and they have.

Whatever was decided, they'd decide together.

"That sound like a plan? My promise."

"Yes," Simon said. He looked at his sister. "As long as we decide together."

Christie took a deep breath, a moment passed, knowing she meant what she said.

"But first, I'll need to—"

A knock on the door, then the doctor walked in, still looking as rumpled as he had the night before.

"Hi."

Though clearly fatigued, he too smiled at her kids. "Can we talk a bit?"

He looked at the kids. Then added, "Need to talk to your mom about her wound, okay? Take a look at it. Maybe you can wait back in your room?"

Kate answered for the two of them.

"Yes. Mom, we'll come back later. Stay with you."

"I'd like that."

And Kate and Simon walked out as the doctor walked over to the bed, his eyes hooded, bloodshot, the fatigue palpable.

"Let's start by taking a look at the wound, hmm?"

And the doctor slowly pulled back the bed sheets.

5
What's Going on Here?

For a long time, the doctor didn't say anything, even when—gloves on—he peeled back the bandage. Only when Karen came in did he say, "Can we get another trauma bandage ready? Thanks."

And the nurse bustled out as fast as she entered.

Until finally Christie had to say, "So?"

The doctor looked up from the wound on her right thigh to Christie's face, and smiled. "Looks good. With all your blood loss, seemed bad, worse than it really was. Stitches look clean, and the bandage is doing its job. I'm happy."

Karen came in with another bandage pack, a puffy plastic bag with the self-contained bandage, probably loaded with antibiotics and—she hoped—a local aesthetic.

"Much pain during the night?" Dr. Martin asked.

"No. I mean, if I move it, feel the pull."

"Yeah. You will have that for a few days. Should be a little better each day."

He ripped open the bandage pack, and then carefully placed the pad on the wound, just above where the stitches ended.

"I need to clean up the suture with hydrogen peroxide... that will sting. But as I said, I'm happy. Mending well already."

Christie watched as he took a swab, dipped it into a vial and applied the peroxide right to the stitches, and the skin around the wound.

A slight sting. Nothing she couldn't handle.

The doctor tended to the wound quietly.

Still—Christie knew that this morning she had questions that weren't just about her wound.

There were a lot of things she needed to know about.

And this was the time.

*

She waited until the doctor had snapped off his gloves and tossed them in a nearby bin.

"Doctor, what is this place?"

He turned to her, smiled. "What do you mean? It's a hospital. Rather obvious, I thought."

She nodded.

Not at all what she meant.

"No. Sure—it's a hospital. But you have people here, staying up at night with guns, guarding. People—I guess—living here."

He didn't say anything.

"But I've been out there; I know what's happened... what's happening. How can you keep this place running? What are you going to do with all the people? Feed them? Care for them?"

She wondered if he knew that she was asking the question not out of any idle interest, but because she was here, her kids were *here*.

She *had* to know.

The doctor looked at the open door of the room and then, without a word, walked over and shut it.

Then he grabbed a straight-backed chair and pulled it close to the bed, sat down.

"Okay. Right. When things got bad out there, the past few months, worse than before..." He took a breath. "When nobody knew where the hell the troopers were, when the attacks kept coming... so many people ended up here. We were swamped."

Another breath.

"We *are* swamped."

"I'm sure."

"The fence—that had been taken care of years ago, along with our generator. Though fuel remains a problem. Always scavenging for that. And food, supplies. No choice really. For the people here, there was nowhere to go back to. Homes gone, neighbors dead—the ones that hadn't changed, that is. This became a safe place."

A safe place.

She had heard that term before.

"You took people in, even after you took care of their wounds?"

"Yes. Had to. I mean, what else could we do?"

Christie nodded.

"And the other doctors?"

At that, Dr. Martin shook his head, looking so weary.

"Oh, you mean the medical staff here? I'm afraid you're looking at it."

"Just you?"

A nod. "We *had* others. Many left to get to their families. Some said they'd be back but never came back. We have two nurses. Karen, and another young woman, Emma, who really is more of an EMT. She stays with the kids mostly."

Then she asked the difficult question.

"What's the plan?"

That stopped the doctor. "Plan? I guess, hang on here, take care of people. People go out for supplies, though with winter coming that won't be easy. Stay alive. What's the phrase? One day at a time."

Christie thought of their family home on Staten Island, inside the safe, secure development girded by a massive electric fence.

Safe. Then, completely overrun, taken over by hordes of Can Heads.

And the Mountain Inn. What did they call it? *A redoubt.* A mountain fortress, and yet it still was besieged by Can Heads.

That is... until it was attacked by something new.

By people who seemed perfectly normal.

By people that were more terrifying than the cannibalistic monsters that roamed the surrounding woods.

Did the doctor know of such things?

"Doctor, when we—my kids, myself—left that mountain inn, I had seen something. Haven't even talked to my kids about."

"Go on."

"People. Looking just like you and me. Who went out… they went out…"

She started to shake, the memory of what she witnessed suddenly hitting her so hard.

"…captured others."

"For what reason?"

He didn't know? He couldn't *goddamn* guess?

Christie had to tell the doctor that things were actually worse than he imagined.

She struggled to control her emotions; she slowed down her speech.

"They collected *children*. They herded them, Doctor. Ready to take them with them, wherever they went."

Did he understand? Did she have to spell it out for him?

Because if she did, Christie felt as if she would lose it.

But then the doctor said, "God. How can that be?"

"Because it *is*. I don't know. Maybe it's part of this whole plague; maybe it's something new. Or maybe it's just about survival."

Then her point.

The one that made her stomach tighten, especially now with her confined to bed.

"Your people here. Could it happen to any of them? Could any of them, all those people with their big guns, could they get that idea? In the interest of surviving."

The doctor shook his head, clearly rattled.

But Christie could see in his eyes that he could well imagine the terror she was talking about.

Maybe had even seen some signs of it already.

But then he said, "I think we're okay... the people here, with their kids. Good people..."

"We were all 'good people' once."

Finally the doctor turned away. "I... I've got other patients. The only doctor, right? 'Rounds,' they used to call them."

He stood up and pushed the chair against the wall.

"Maybe we can talk some more. Let's see how the healing goes, hmm?"

Christie nodded.

"I'll check in later. You should sleep, rest as much as you can."

But in a painful move, Christie leaned up, using one arm. She had to make a point. She had to ask one more thing.

"I will. But can you check on my kids? During the day. Make sure they're okay." A deep breath, hoping that the man knew what she was asking.

To keep his eyes open. For anything. Because Christie couldn't.

"Can you do that?"

The doctor nodded. "I will. And Karen, she's tireless. My right arm. I will ask her as well. We'll keep eyes on them, talk to them."

Christie lowered herself back down to the pillow, grateful for the promise.

"And you just work on getting better, okay?"

Christie smiled at that.

She closed her eyes as he left the room, and in seconds she was dead asleep again.

6
Days and Nights

"Simon! What are you *doing?*"

Kate had frozen as Simon turned a corner to a far hallway that led to the back of the hospital building.

One of the men had been very clear: "You don't go past that point. *Ever.*"

Then, as if threatening, he had looked right at Kate. "You got that?"

She had nodded.

But after two days here, wandering on the only floor they were allowed on, only part of the first floor of the hospital, wandering back and forth, down the few corridors here that were permitted, she could see Simon wanting to...

What?

Explore?

Her brother turned. Since the events from nights before, he had been good about listening to her. Once—and it nearly made her cry, so stupid—he even said to her, *"Kate. What you did. Saving me and all? Thanks."*

She was quick to say it was nothing. *"Just stopped those creepy men, Simon. That's all."*

And he had added without thinking: *"And I'd do the same for you."*

That was chilling. Knowing that he meant that. And more—

that after all that had happened—was there anyone better to have her back than Simon?

Now that her Mom was laid up.

Simon had stopped, just at the turn in the hallway.

"Now you see me…" he said, grinning.

Then he slid a few feet to his right, and vanished.

Kate stood there, suspended. She didn't want to chase after him, go where the men said not to go.

Though who knows why they said that.

Why can't we walk around the whole building? At least in daylight? All locked up, the gates working.

Why is that so bad?

"Simon!" she said, even louder, and quickly spun around to see if anyone heard. But all she saw was an old man in a walker, slowly trudging in her direction, his head down.

If Simon didn't come back, she'd have to go get him.

And if the men found them, what would they do?

Yell at them? Lock them up?

Mom doesn't need anything else to worry about.

She decided she had no choice. If Simon was going to be stupid, back to being a stupid boy who did what he wanted to, then she'd have to go get him—and fast.

She hurried down the hallway, glancing every few steps over her shoulder to see if anyone was watching, until… she reached the turn, took the turn, and saw that…

Simon hadn't gone far at all.

*

He stood only feet away, looking straight down the other hallway. To the right, Kate saw doors to what appeared to be a stairway. A heavy chain with locks surrounded the two doors' handles.

And next to the doors, an elevator, door open, and a heavy chair sitting across the entrance as if letting anyone know, *Don't go into this elevator.*

Don't move the chair.

Something felt so bad about seeing those two things.

But worse, when she turned and saw what Simon was looking at, what had stopped him cold.

Halfway down the next hallway, she saw... what? A jumble of chairs, and dozens of metal poles, piled seven, eight feet high, right to the ceiling.

Like a crazy arts and crafts project.

It's a barrier, she thought. *A wall.*

And why would they have a wall in *here?*

The hospital was safe. The fence, all those guns.

Simon must have sensed he wasn't alone, and when he turned back to her, he wasn't grinning.

No. Kate knew that after what they had seen, they could look at such a thing—and guess what it meant.

It didn't need to be said.

And she hoped that Simon wouldn't say it. Because it would make it all too real.

The message of that wall...

They have gotten in here. There have been battles in here.

And the people with their guns, even some girls not much older than her, must know that message.

The message:

We're not safe here.

Simon walked back. She almost wished he was still grinning at his rule breaking. Instead, that grin was all gone.

And it was Simon who said, so quietly, "We better walk back."

Kate turned, and with no more words, followed her brother back to the other corridors, to the ER, to all the people.

Guns ready. Waiting.

Waiting.

*

35

At lunch—a pasty mix of something green, something like potatoes, probably instant—they sat alone.

No one had come over and talked to them.

Newcomers to this place weren't welcome.

And these days, Kate knew why.

More mouths. More need for food.

She took a spoonful of the greenish mixture, heavily salted, and that just about made it edible.

Simon wasn't eager to eat and quickly put down his spoon. He leaned close to Kate.

"Kate."

She knew this was coming. Simon would want to talk about what they saw.

And this was as close to privacy as they could get. Even when they visited their mother, the nurse was constantly bustling in and out, ready to hear whatever they were talking about.

She nodded at her brother. "Yeah."

"We *can't* stay here."

Another nod.

Then as if what he said wasn't clear enough. "We have to get out of here. Everyone here"—a look around—"is just waiting for an attack."

He had raised his voice. Kate leaned close. "Quiet, will you? Just whisper."

And now Simon nodded, but Kate guessed she better say something. Because if she knew anything about her brother, when he had an idea he didn't let it go.

What was that word?

Tenacious.

"Okay. Maybe it's not good here, and—"

"Maybe?"

"And okay—we shouldn't stay here."

"That pile of junk," Simon said. "Sooner or later, they'll get back in." He took a breath. "I don't want to be here when that happens, Kate."

She looked at him. Just a kid, not even a teenager yet, but his words made him sound like... if he had to, he'd go off on his own.

She even had to wonder: *He wouldn't really do that, would he?*

"I know," she said. "But Mom needs to get better, I don't know how many more days she needs. Tomorrow the doctor told her she can try to walk, get some strength back."

"How long will it take? Until she can leave? Until *we* can leave?"

"I don't *know*, Simon. I'm not a doctor. Look, we're supposed to visit her after lunch. Maybe we can talk then. Plan."

Simon looked around.

Then he turned back to his sister and finally she saw a bit of a smile bloom on his face.

"You know, you weren't too bad at driving. I mean, if that's what has to happen. For us to leave."

She smiled back. "I wasn't, was I? And you know what, it was kinda fun."

Simon kept smiling, their meeting over. This serious chat about such serious things.

Like getting out before an attack.

Would their mom want to hear about this, when she was still recovering?

Doubtful. But no matter. They were together. And if it was time to talk, time to plan, then that's what it was.

She looked down at her plate of goop. She knew that she couldn't dump it. Throwing away food, even when it was this disgusting, wouldn't be welcome.

"Let's finish eating this great stuff and go see Mom."

"Yum!" Simon said, his smile twisted into a grimace that made Kate laugh.

And did that ever feel good.

7
Plans

Kate led the way into her mom's room, and saw an empty bed. Simon nearly collided into her.

Then they both looked to the window where their mother was standing, holding one of those metal walkers that old people use, and then—with a smile— started shuffling toward them.

Steps away, the nurse, Karen, looked on, a big smile on her face as well. Kate led the way into her mom's room, and saw an empty bed. Simon nearly collided into her.

Then they both looked to the window where their mother was standing, holding one of those metal walkers that old people use, and then—with a smile—started shuffling toward them.

Steps away, the nurse, Karen, looked on, a big smile on her face as well.

"You're up," Kate said, pointing out the obvious.

"She's doing great!" Karen said.

"Little tricky," her mom said as she lifted the walker a bit and took some more steps. "Bit of practice, and I think I might manage with just a cane."

Simon walked over to his mother. And Kate was suddenly afraid that he would tell their mother now what they had seen.

While Kate felt that it was best they talked about it when they were alone.

Just the three of them.

"That's great, Mom," Kate said fast as if that might keep Simon quiet.

But then with a glance from her brother, nodding toward the nurse, his lips tight, she knew she didn't have anything to worry about.

He didn't say a thing. Just smiled as his mother closed the distance to one end of the room, and then turned.

"Now, don't overdo it," Karen said. "A few more 'laps' then back to bed. Still healing, you know…"

Christie nodded, then, after one step, now closer, Kate looked right at her.

A silent message.

That Kate was sure her mother got.

We need to talk.

Alone.

Christie turned to the nurse. "Think I'll stop for now. More later, okay? And now a little visit with my kids."

Karen nodded.

"Sure. Maybe a walk down the hallway before dinner?"

"Great."

Karen smiled, looking from Christie to Kate… Simon.

Then left the room.

The door open.

Kate walked over to the door—waited a few moments, and then gently pushed it shut tight.

*

Christie sat on the bed, Simon sitting close, Kate standing.

My big girl, she thought.

"Looks like you're doing good, Mom," she said.

And Christie thought, *She didn't shut the door to tell me that.*

"Least I can move. Healing is going well. Yeah, so not bad."

Quiet then. Christie looked at Simon, whose eyes were trained on his sister.

Until Christie had to say: "Okay. What's up?"

Kate nodded.

"Down the hallway, at the other end..."

"Where we weren't supposed to go," Simon added.

Where of course he went.

"We saw something." He took a breath. "It was scary, Mom."

Christie nodded. She had talked to the doctor about this hospital. What was going on.

More importantly: How it could *keep* going on. All these people, holed up here, hiding.

"What did you see?"

And now Simon slid off the bed.

"It was a wall. Made out of things like"—and he pointed to the metal pole that held her IV drip, now no longer needed—"those things. And chairs. A big wall, a pile of junk."

"Like it was made to keep things out," Kate added.

Christie nodded. She could guess what that "wall" was, and what it meant.

This place, with its fence, not always secure.

It had been attacked, and it could be again.

Christie cleared her throat. "I understand."

She didn't know what to say. She had hoped she could recover here, get stronger. For the past few days, that had been her only thought—that and the idea that her kids were safe here.

But that wall meant something else.

"Mom—we don't think we should stay here much longer," Kate said.

"Any," Simon added.

Christie turned to him.

"Any longer," Simon said. Then, after he looked away, "I got a bad feeling, Mom."

And after what Simon had been through, how could she ignore his feelings?

At that moment, before she could respond to her son, the door opened. Karen stuck her head in. "All good?"

Christie smiled, nodded.

Wondering whether Karen had any idea what this "meeting" was about.

"Just wanted to let you know that the doctor will be by in a bit, check things. I told him you're doing great with the walker. Maybe can use a cane soon."

Christie forced a smile. "Thanks."

Karen nodded and then, maybe—Christie thought—sensing that the door had been shut for a reason, the nurse backed out and shut the door tightly behind her.

Kate took a step closer.

Her voice a whisper.

"Mom. We need to plan."

Simon nodded.

Christie looked at the two of them. She had told them that they would be doing things, deciding things—whatever happened—together. And while she had hoped she could have gotten a few more days to *not* think about things, that wasn't going to happen.

"Okay. Let's talk. Just like we agreed."

She took Kate's left hand, steering her to sit on her left.

Then Simon's right hand as well, holding it tight.

"What do you two... think?"

Kate took the lead, telling Christie about the wall of chairs, tables, metal at the end of the hall. "I'm guessing there's been break-ins."

"Could be. At least one, I guess," Christie said.

"Maybe more, Mom," Simon added. "No one has told us that though. Pretty sure people here aren't too happy we're here."

She turned to her son.

"What do you mean?"

"Dunno. But the looks they give us? Like they wish we'd just go away."

"The nurse, Karen… she's nice," Kate added quickly. "But, yeah, well… people look at us."

Kate nodded.

Christie could have suspected that.

With everything scarce: food, supplies, weapons and ammo… the stuff of life these days. All in limited supply. Newcomers would definitely be unwelcome.

The big question: how unwelcome?

"Okay, Sorry, kids you had to, um, deal with that. I just had hoped… while I got better…"

Now Simon took over. "Mom. We don't think this is a good place to be when they come."

"The Can Heads," she said.

"Yes," Simon said. "But the others too. They're out there somewhere. Those people how they caught me… who had me in a noose, caught…"

She thought for a moment that Simon was about to crack. His eyes glistened, and she felt that there was nothing she could do to stem the tears.

Her own throat tightened.

They hadn't talked about that night.

Not yet.

Now they sat, the three of them talking quietly.

Plotting, she thought.

Because that's what they were doing. The three of them, alone, trying to figure out what to do.

"But there's a fence, kids. That big electric fence."

Christie squeezed her kids' hands.

Kate shook her head. "Then what about the wall we saw, Mom? If that fence always works, if it's always dependable, why is that whole side of the building closed?"

"It's like…" And now Simon slid off the bed, freeing himself from his mother's handhold. "…they're all hiding here, just waiting for the next attack."

He turned and looked right at her, seeming so much not like a boy.

He's changed, she thought.

His voice so serious, his meaning clear.

"And we can't do that." A breath. "We can't hide."

She looked at Kate. Maybe her daughter better understood how long it takes to fully recuperate, understood that Christie would want some more time.

But Christie meant what she had told them. If there was one thing they could depend upon, it was her promises, their trust in her.

She had to hold true to that.

"Okay. The doctor's coming in soon. Let me talk to him... about how I'm doing. About what we might do..."

"When we can *leave* here," Simon said.

Christie nodded. "That too. 'Cause... well, we can't just leave. I mean, to just go out there. I mean, we need to figure out where to go, what we will do."

Another moment where she came close to losing it.

"You saw our home, our development. That's gone. We have to have a place we're going if we leave, right?"

Kate nodded. Simon didn't seem so sure.

"I guess so," he said. "But if we know we shouldn't stay here, then does it really matter if we know where we're going?"

Christie took a breath.

Her son's logic amazing.

And grim.

"Okay, you two. Let's... not get ahead of ourselves. Let me talk to the doctor, try to learn what I can about what's been going on here, and outside."

"Then we leave... soon," Simon said.

Christie smiled at him. "Then... we come up with a *plan,*" she said. "May take a few days. Do you think you can just—I don't know—be okay for those days? Be patient?"

She looked especially at Kate. There could be special dangers for a teenage girl in a place like this.

No matter how nice the doctor and his nurse seemed.

Which meant... they might not have a lot of time.

"That sound all right?"

Then—an amazing moment—Kate looked at Simon, and they nodded to each other.

The two of them, who used to fight over just about anything.

How she wished for all that bickering to come back.

"Okay," Kate said. Then her daughter smiled. "Good to see you walking, Mom. Keep getting better."

"Doing my best," Christie said. "Now I think I'll lie down."

She nodded. "Come on, Simon."

They walked out of the room, now leaving the door open a crack.

And Christie lay back in the bed.

Not so much in need of rest, as time to think.

The question huge, overwhelming...

What do we do?

What the hell... do we do?

8
A Bedside Chat

Christie opened her eyes and saw Dr. Martin, clipboard in hand, standing beside the bed.

"Doctor," she said.

She realized that even the small amount of walking she had done had taken a toll and that she might not be as strong as she thought she was.

Still, as she promised her kids, she'd have to have this conversation.

"Ah, awake. Hear you've been tearing up and down with the walker. Good to hear. Let me look at the wound and see how that's doing, hmm?"

Christie nodded.

The doctor seemed so warm, reassuring… a character out of a Norman Rockwell painting, an old-time doctor of a type that she would have thought had vanished a long time ago.

But then she remembered that all the other doctors from this place had indeed vanished.

This Dr. Martin had to be a very special breed.

It made her think that maybe she'd like to stay here longer.

But then, she didn't know what it was like outside the hospital room doors, out with the other people, getting looks, being the "unwelcome visitors."

He peeled back the blanket and sheet, and then looked down at the bandage.

"Don't want to remove it completely. Not if all's good. Just want to take a look at the stitches… so here we go."

She felt the adhesive pull at her skin.

The doctor nodded, then up to her face. "Looks great. Never was the best one for knitting things up, but must say… not too bad. And it's not wet, dry and healing's going well." A nod, the doctor pleased to pass on the news. "All good."

He pressed the bandage back into place. "We'll change it this evening. Fresh compress… maybe something smaller."

He pulled the blanket and sheet up and started to turn away.

"Doctor," Christie said.

He stopped, turned in place.

Had to be other people here who needed his attention. Kids with colds, pregnant women, people who had been hurt… attacked just getting here.

Only one man, and probably so much to do.

Still, "Can I talk to you a bit?"

He didn't immediately nod or smile. But Christie watched him narrow his eyes, a wise look that suggested to her that maybe he knew what was about to come.

Finally he said, "Sure. Of course."

He pulled a chair close to the bed. He too glanced at the open door but didn't shut it.

After all, he didn't know what she was going to talk about.

"Doctor, I wonder… I've been talking with my kids. And just wondering about things…"

A small nod.

Suggesting… *go on.*

So she did.

"About this place, the hospital. Everyone here. Just wondering about how safe we are."

She waited, thinking that he would immediately offer

reassurances.

Instead, this doctor who seemed so warm, chatty even, was quiet.

"About the danger here."

She wondered if he knew she was referring to *all* kinds of danger, and not just the packs of Can Heads prowling outside.

Then, "Ask away."

She described the "wall" that her kids had seen, and what it obviously meant.

And then, a bit harder to say, how her kids felt those looks from people making them feel unwanted.

The doctor rubbed his chin, weighing his words.

"I do… what I can here, Christie. The thing I was trained for, hmm? Help people"—A smile now—"repair them, just like I did with your leg. Deal with everything that comes here… that's what a doctor does. And I do it here because it's a hospital, yes? We have rooms, beds, some medicine—though the supplies get less and less."

Christie tried to figure out where he was going with this.

"So, you ask about safety? And I frankly don't know what to tell you. Yes, we've been attacked. That pile of junk, that 'wall,' was made after the last one. The fence went down, and in they came. Lost people that night. But that was over a month ago. Now we have backups. I think…"

Hesitation there, as if he really didn't believe it.

"…*think* we're safer now."

"And the people here?"

"Hmm?"

"How safe are they?"

No smile now.

"The people here, they're all types. Like any community of people just… thrown together. Technically, this is still a hospital, so maybe I should be in charge."

A beat.

"But I'm not. A group of men seems to run things, not that

anyone elected them.”

“So… outside this room, it’s a different world?”

“Yes. And I’m not saying it’s not safe here, for you, your kids. It’s a world of people just trying to stay alive in the face of something they don’t understand.”

“They’re afraid.”

“Exactly. And we know what fear can do.”

Christie thought over his words before continuing.

Then, “Thank you for answering my questions. I’m thinking that… as soon as possible… it might be best if my kids and I leave.”

Another squint, the doctor in the room not liking that.

“You still have healing to do, more rehabilitation. I think any thought of that, any discussion… well, it’s not for now.”

And then Christie got a sense that there was something that he hadn’t told her, that now he was about to tell her.

Then, he did. “I have a question for you.”

Christie’s turn to nod.

“Were you a runner?”

“Um, before kids, yes, I always ran, even the early years. Did 5Ks, even a few longer races.”

“I imagined as much.”

“And we had a treadmill. Jack didn’t like the idea of me running around our neighborhood. Though it seemed perfectly safe, he always said…”

He always said.

And she could hear his voice, so strong, so straight, so clear in her ears. And it was almost too much.

She waited a moment.

A breath.

“I ran on the treadmill. Tried to stay fit. Really important, especially after everything changed.”

“After the Can Heads…”

Then the doctor looked down at Christie’s leg, as if he needed say nothing more.

"What is it?" she asked.

"Even after you heal, even after your leg is all better, there's been muscle damage. Also, some nerve damage. It will heal, but…"

She could figure out the rest.

"You're saying… I won't ever run again?"

A nod. "In a bigger hospital, we could do advanced tissue work, perhaps give you better mobility. But here, with what we have, I can get you walking—"

"You already have."

A smile. "Yes. But you won't be able to run with that leg. I just needed you to know that."

And Christie nodded, though she had only started to process what the doctor's words meant.

In this world, not be able to run, what did that mean?

What could that mean?

Can Heads could be so fast. Those people that she saw herding children.

Children.

They could easily outrun her.

Slowly, the meaning of Dr. Martin's words was sinking in. She would have a vulnerability that—in this world—could mean the difference between life and death.

And then, an odd thought. The old DVD set she and Jack had watched. He was always a history buff and, with her being a history teacher, it was that subject that brought them together.

Had to be unusual for an NYPD cop.

And they watched the mammoth series on the Roosevelts.

But they were most engrossed by the incredible story of FDR, his battle against a crippling disease that should have eliminated him from any chance of being president.

Immobilized by polio, and yet he would be the leader to rally the nation to act to stop what seemed the inevitable Nazi Empire.

They told him he'd never walk again.

Just like she had just been told: *You will never run again.*

And yet, in a fashion, with difficulty, he walked.

To inspire a nation, never yielding to his disease, not when the world needed all he could give.

Just like my kids, she thought.

They need so much from me.

They may need to hear what she has just learned. But they will also need to know that she will do whatever she can to overcome that challenge.

Whatever it would take.

It was a discussion that would have to happen. But not today, not tomorrow. But eventually.

Because, she thought, *not having that speed to run could force terrible choices on all of them.*

With that thought, she shivered.

"Cold?" the doctor said.

She shook her head even as she pulled the blanket closer to her neck.

"I'm okay. And thank you for telling me. It's something I needed to know."

The doctor smiled. "And it's nothing you need to deal with—or think about—until you get much better. Just want you to…"

He stood up.

"…continue the good work you've been doing here, hmm?"

She heard in his voice that the idea of them leaving lay in some distant future.

She'd have to tell the kids that. They'd have to be patient.

They'd simply have to give her and her wound a little more time.

At least… that's what she thought she'd be telling them.

But plans, she had learned, could always change.

"Rest up," Dr. Martin said, leaving the room.

And with serious things to consider, to weigh, Christie shut her eyes.

Dinner soon, and then, coming so early, a wintry darkness. A

moonless night.
    And that fact seemed important.
    And it was.

9
Night—Part One

"Let's get out of here," Simon said.

Kate saw that her brother had hardly put a dent in whatever glop constituted dinner tonight.

She leaned forward so she'd only be heard by him, though no one had even tried to sit near them.

But Kate certainly felt the eyes of some of the men—all different ages—on her as she slowly spooned the soupy dinner into her mouth.

"Simon, you need to finish that."

Simon looked down at his plate.

"This stuff *sucks.*"

It was actually funny the way he said it. But his boldness, and the fact that he was not whispering, also worried her.

"Simon, they won't be happy if you don't finish it all. Food's precious. If we waste it, then…"

He used his spoon to make a rounded pile float in the air, then with a tilt, let it slip off the spoon onto the larger mound on the plate.

"This is food?"

She grinned at that.

Except… now was not the time.

"Please, just eat it, then we can see Mom."

"Right. And try to stay out of everyone's way." Then he looked around. "I hate this place."

"We've talked about this. You know—"

"Okay, okay." And he dug his spoon into the food and with dopey grin began eating it as fast as he could. "Yum!"

*

A man walked into Christie's room without knocking.

"Here for the tray," he said.

He had a gun slung over his shoulder. Rumpled jeans, stained flannel shirt.

Guess everyone pitches in here.

Which is what she would need do as well.

That is, if they ended up staying.

"Thanks," she said, to which the man said nothing. He just grabbed the tray and walked out.

Nice talking to you as well.

She felt a bit of what her kids must be experiencing.

Such a cutting coldness.

And then Kate and Simon came in, Simon plopping on the bed with a thump that showed that he wasn't terribly aware of her healing wound.

Kate stood by the bed.

"Ate all my dinner!" Simon said. "Isn't that right, Kate?"

She saw her daughter nod, then roll her eyes. Kate these days being sister, stand-in mom, and maybe—Christie guessed—guardian.

"That he did. Though not before saying pretty loudly that it 'sucks.'"

"'Cause it did. You have that same stuff, Mom? Gross."

Actually, Christie didn't think it was much worse than the meals she patched together back in their home on Staten Island.

"Was filling at least," she said.

Simon patted his belly. "Yup, sure is. I'm full of the gloppy stuff now."

And then—amazing moment—all three of them laughed.

Looking at each other, *laughing.*

As if that was somehow impossible.

And when the laughing stopped, they talked—not about anything important, not about the future. But about the people here, how long and boring the days were... before Christie suggested checking out the room's TV that, in the evening, showed DVDs.

Tonight, it was *E.T.*

Perfect, Christie thought. Especially when they sat close and got lost in the plight of a little alien gardener who just...

And this would always make her cry at the end. How could it not?

...just... wanted to go home.

*

A small nightlight sat below Christie's hospital bed.

But the large flood lights that covered the fence and parking lot outside made the windows—even with blinds closed—glow brightly.

Each night, she woke a couple of times.

Parched, she guessed, needing a sip of the now-tepid water. Or maybe tossing in the bed, and triggering a little pull on her right leg, on the bandage, and her eyes would open wide.

Each night, the same thing.

Now she woke up, not sure why. She saw the bright, milky light from outside, the small glow below her bed.

But she noticed something.

Not thirsty.

And her leg felt fine.

She just *woke up.*

But this felt familiar.

Like the way she used to wake up when Jack worked nights, when she was alone with the kids—and suddenly alert as she strained to catch every sound inside and outside the house.

Alert to anything that... shouldn't be there.

This was exactly like that.

Then, she thought she heard a noise outside. Faint sounds. Movement. Then—just barely heard—a hacking cough.

Just people outside.

She closed her eyes.

Nothing.

She just woke up for some reason. Who knew why?

And then—even with her eyes tightly shut, struggling to keep out the glow from the window, the massive floods outside—the light vanished.

All the light was gone.

Her eyes shot open again.

Christie lay in the darkness. A total darkness, nothing from outside now, the big lights dark on this moonless night.

And the little glow below her bed—also gone.

Now she easily heard voices, people outside, in the corridor. Not making out the words, but the tone so clear. Excitement, panic, yells.

Her heart raced. The lights were off.

Because...

Because...

The power was down. Had to be! And if the power was down, then the fence was dead. Yes, and could easily be climbed over.

Christie raised herself up using her elbows, not that she could see anything, do anything.

The voices outside continued until...

With a *POP*, the lights came back on, and her room was again bathed by the brilliant white stripes that cut into the hospital room. The small night light just to the side of the headboard, also on.

Right. The generator came on. Or maybe the backup. Nothing to worry about.

But then, she heard other sounds from outside. A howling, an animal sound... then a terrible crackling noise almost as loud as the pained howls.

She could guess what that was.

Some of them—the Can Heads who gathered at night—had jumped onto the fence.

And now, power back on, they were pinned to that fence as the electricity coursed through their bodies, killing them, cooking them.

Somehow the thought of them being killed wasn't comforting at all.

But at least the lights were back on, power restored, and the voices in the corridor suddenly calmed.

And then—when that thought should have brought peace, should have made her heart stop racing so fast—the lights went off again.

Only now, they stayed off.

Christie tried counting.

Some magical process that might hasten the generator kicking in again. Her slow counting matched to steady breathing that somehow was supposed to bring the power back.

By the time she got to twenty.

Then:

Okay, to thirty.

Thirty-five... forty.

Soon.

The room remained as black as a closet sealed tight.

She heard gunshots. So many guns firing, over and over.

Into the darkness, she thought.

The people out there firing into the pitch-black darkness.

She knew what she had to do now. Because this wasn't simply about her being stranded in this dark room.

My kids are out there somewhere.

Their brief respite from the madness of this world suddenly over.

She kicked the covers off, the sheet. Then she slowly swung her legs around. Bare feet touched the chilly linoleum floor. Slippers somewhere, but how could she find them?

Her hospital gown absurdly cold.

And as she stuck out her hands to search for the door out of the room, each icy step seemed matched to the gunshots.

Then yells.

No. Screams.

God. Screams.

She banged into a wall, then with another step her left foot rammed into the leg of a chair.

But she hurried, stumbling, fast as she could.

Thinking... *screams.*

10
Night—Part Two

"Simon!" Kate said in the darkness.

His answer steady. Only feet away, but the darkness making his voice seem as though it came from a deep well to nowhere.

"Simon. You okay?"

He didn't say anything.

"Simon!"

"Kate. What happened? They said they had—"

"I know, I know. A backup generator."

"We can't just *sit* here."

She heard movement, Simon out of his bed. The rattle of a belt buckle. Simon getting dressed in the dark.

Kate didn't know what to do. The gunshots outside sounded like firecrackers shooting, random, sporadic. Over and over, matched to the voices—men mostly, but also women.

Yelling, barking words.

She knew Simon was right.

She too slid out of bed and started getting dressed, picking up jeans, a sweater, then using a foot to feel around for her sneakers.

"I'm going out there," Simon said.

"No," Kate said, stupidly shaking her head. "Wait for me. Just a minute."

But—in the darkness—the door opened. She felt a draft as she

58

nudged one sneaker, then bent down and began unlacing it so she could put it on.

Why did I do that? she thought. *Should always leave them unlaced. Should always be ready.*

And when she had both sneakers on, feet sockless since the socks seemed to have rolled away into nowhere, she started toward the open door now tinged with a bit of reflective light.

Flashlights outside.

Just enough to see.

She thought of Simon. And then her mother.

Thinking: *What should I do?*

*

Simon stopped as soon as he got to the hallway. He could see the entrance lobby down at the other end.

And the people there had flashlights all pointed out at the door and windows, just a bit of light outlining the people crouched there.

But enough light, so that Simon could see the cloud of smoke hanging over them as they kept on firing.

Then two dark shadows ran toward Simon.

For a moment he thought that they were coming for him. But after nearly smashing into him, at the last moment one cut left, the other to Simon's right, racing down the hallway.

I know where they're going, thought Simon.

To the wall, to the far end of the long corridor.

Where that wall of junk was supposed to stop them.

But with the fence down, with all this darkness, could they be stopped?

Then he had the strangest thought.

Only months ago it would have seemed so... crazy. Now, it made perfect sense.

That thought...

I need to get my gun from them.

He started walking down the hallway, his eyes locked on the

barely lit mass of people shooting and shooting and shooting.

*

Kate hit the corridor and didn't see her brother. Her mother's room was down in the other direction, farther into the darkness.

Is that where he went?

Too dark to see anything.

Or did Simon go up *there*, where everyone was fighting…

The invasion?

For a moment she was paralyzed, unable to decide.

And then, she spun around, and—arms out to her side so she could feel a wall if she got close—she slowly made her way to her mother's room.

*

Christie turned around, staring into the darkness of the hallway. Gunshots echoed from down there as well.

Both ends of this corridor under siege.

And all she could think about were her kids. But even with that driving her, it took only a few steps, holding on to the nearest wall, for the pain in her leg to intensify.

The walker had been left behind, forgotten in her panic.

She thought of yelling, calling out their names, but the explosive echo of the gunshots would make that pointless.

Another painful step in the dark, toward the distant light of the lobby area with flashes of the gunshots and the reflection of flashlights, both pointed at the enemy outside.

Then, another step, eyes watering.

Only this time someone fell into her, and Christie reeled back, starting to tumble to the ground.

When that same person grabbed her and stopped the fall.

"Mom!"

Despite the pain, Christie felt as if she had just been given a gift.

"Kate! Kate, you're okay. What's going on?"

Such a stupid question. Silly. It was obvious what was going on.

"They're attacking. Something happened to the electricity, the fence."

Which now meant, Christie knew, that this building had just turned into a terrible trap.

Then, even as she was so glad to have her daughter helping her stand, supporting her, "Simon? Where's Simon?"

"I-I don't know!"

Christie's voice turned harsh. She asked so much of Kate, but that was the way it had to be.

"You don't know where your brother is?"

"It was so dark. He left the room. I thought he came down here to you."

Christie felt as if she was about to bark at her daughter again. But she knew that was the fear now coursing through her.

She took a breath, as much to calm herself as for the pain.

"Okay, we... we have to find him. He didn't come to me, so he must have... gone down there."

She couldn't see her daughter's face, just felt her arms helping her stand, Kate's voice close.

"I know. But you shouldn't walk down there."

Christie was about to argue, to demand that Kate get her the hell down there.

But then—another breath, another thought—and she knew she was right.

"All right. You're right. But you have to—"

"I will, Mom, I'll get him, bring him back to you. But you should stay in your room."

And Christie had another thought.

My gun.

Taken in the frantic minutes when they came into the hospital. Now leaving her even more defenseless than her weakened leg.

Kate had pivoted her and started the walk back to the room.

"Kate, you need to get a gun. Somehow. Ask someone…"

Though Christie knew that the people here—like people everywhere—would be reluctant to return a weapon. Weapons, ammunition. As important as air and water.

So sick, she thought.

"I will, Mom. I'll find Simon, get a weapon, come back."

They reached the door to the room, the only open door, the door's outline barely visible due to the light outside made by the battery of flashlights trained on the attackers.

As Christie hobbled back to the bed, her eyes were on the window.

Just a window, she thought

An ordinary window that could break, could be smashed.

She'd be sitting here, alone, hoping Kate would be okay, hoping that she'd find Simon, and somehow—what, like magic?—get a weapon for them.

Kate eased her down.

"Go," she said. "I'm fine. Just go now."

"Yes," Kate said.

And then Christie felt that terrible moment when her daughter's hands came off her, that human contact with her child, now a woman… gone.

But Christie thought only one thing.

Hurry, Kate, Hurry.

11
Night Ends

Kate ran down the hallway.

If there were someone racing her way, she wouldn't see them, and they'd easily collide.

Still, she ran.

And in her careening race toward the lobby, she kept her hands out to each side to guide her, to keep her going straight down the hallway.

But as she got closer, the fighting ahead, the people shooting— and what they were doing—became clearer.

Everyone packed tightly together, shooting out into the darkness while others—women and men—held flashlights behind them, pointed out, into that darkness.

The gunfire is constant.

And more steps. She saw a man stand up, and back away, his gun down.

Out of ammo, Kate guessed.

She saw a woman slide into his place and begin shooting as he stepped back, digging in his pockets.

Closer still, and she slowed.

Where was Simon? Where was her brother?

Could something have happened to him?

In just those few minutes… could something bad have happened?

*

Simon stood to the back. The reception desk sat behind him, in front of a big room with glass walls that now reflected the explosive firefly lights made by all the guns.

The smoke cloud made it hard to breathe as it hung over all the people shooting.

No one looked at him. No one said anything.

He looked around.

This isn't everyone.

No, he guessed only the people here were those doing the fighting, and those who held the flashlights pointing outside.

While everyone else hid.

And Simon thought, *Maybe I should be hiding as well?*

Maybe that's all we can do is hide.

One man barked orders, directing people, like the coach of a football team, *"You—go here; and you—over there!"*

Simon kept watching all these people shooting.

Because he didn't really want to look in the other place.

He didn't really want to look outside.

Until he felt that he had to, taking a deep breath even with the gun smoke stinging his eyes, burning his lungs.

He looked out—and saw them.

And... and...

It was like a movie.

So many Can Heads. Some still dressed like ordinary people, with only a few rips and stains on their clothes.

Others naked, their blood-stained bodies lit by the lights, showing wounds, cuts.

As bullets hit them, the Can Heads would reel back.

But—still watching, like it was a show—Simon saw that if it didn't hit them in the head, or the chest, the Can Heads would leap forward, now even more crazed.

They all became like a giant mouth, a living *jaw* of creatures, their hands reaching, their howls as loud as the gunfire.

Until Simon saw a pair of Can Heads leap into the opening together, crashing through the jagged, broken glass of the entrance, and grab a man.

The man standing up, as if surprised. An old guy, gray beard.

Waving his rifle until it fell to the ground as they yanked him out so fast, his gun sliding like a hockey puck across the floor.

And since everyone else had to keep firing, had to keep the lights trained on the Can Heads, the gun slid all the way over.

To the reception desk.

Simon reached down and picked it up.

The old man's weapon, now warm in his hands. A few moments before that man had been firing it, holding it tight.

And now he was out there, lost, vanished.

Devoured.

Now holding the rifle tightly, Simon took a step away from that desk. Toward the army of people fighting the Can Heads.

I have a gun, Simon thought. *I have to help them.*

*

Kate looked at the madness before her.

Did she really just see one of the men in front yanked away, pulled out into the sea of Can Heads outside so fast?

Her stomach tightened; she felt as if she might throw up, dizzy from the smells and the noise.

Simon," she said, a near whisper.

Just for herself. To remind herself about what she was doing here.

Have to find my brother.

Until—a horrible moment—she saw he was one of them... Simon was one of those people shooting.

No.

How long can they do this, she thought? *How long before one side—or the other—wins?*

She made her way closer, ducking under people with lights, no one paying any attention to her at all, no one yelling at her or her brother to get the hell away.

Everyone using all their attention to stay focused on this terrible battle.

Until she stood beside him, and she crouched down.

Simon kept firing.

She noticed that pools of blood seemed to be all over.

Human blood? Can Head blood?

Did it matter?

She leaned close.

"Simon!" she yelled.

And when he didn't seem to pay any attention to her, lost to the battle like all the adults, as if he too was—God—an adult, she yelled his name.

"Simon! Mom's alone! We have to get back to Mom." Then, "With the gun."

Only then did he turn, his eyes glistening, watery from the smoke that filled the night.

"Simon!" she shouted again as loudly as she could. Then, just the one word which she hoped would be enough, would remind him of something important that could get lost in this madness.

"Mom! Mom, Simon!"

A nod. He backed up.

Both of them backing up as she took his hand, no objection to her doing that. More steps, the gun lowered.

And just as no one could pay any attention to their arrival at this stand against the Can Heads, no one noticed when they finally were away from the seething, shooting mass, when they turned and started running back to their mother's room.

And all Kate could think: *Will this night ever end?*

Until, slowing so she didn't miss the open door to her mother's room, they came to her room.

The door open.

She held her breath then.

After all, anything could happen...

And with Simon trailing, she walked in.

"Mom. I found him, and—"

Simon spoke in the darkness.

"I got a gun. I think it still has bullets."

Kate could hear the pride in her brother's voice. And then she had to wonder, *Bullets? How many?*

Would they be enough? Would there ever be enough?

Then, her mother's voice.

"Good. Come closer. Stay with me."

Kate released Simon as she went to the bed.

But her brother went to the window, the closed blinds.

"Simon," her mother said.

She's back in charge, thought Kate.

And that was good.

*

"Simon, come away from the window."

Christie tried to keep her voice gentle, talking to her son holding a rifle.

"Don't let them see that we're here."

Christie could see the bare outline of her son standing by the blinds, a dark shape, on guard. She thought that she might have to repeat the order, but then Simon took a step back.

Now what? Christie thought.

She wanted to ask Kate what was it like, down there where people fought the Can Heads.

But her two kids had seen it. That was enough.

Then, *What do we do now?*

Kate sat close. And with just the distant sound of gunfire, no one said anything for a long time.

12
Doing What Must Be Done

Eventually the gunshots stopped.

The lights flickered on in Christie's hospital room, but by then Kate was asleep next to her.

Simon had also fallen asleep in a tattered reclining chair.

Neither awoke when the room lights came on. Christie used her cane and got to the light switch, shut it off, leaving just the small light on the wall under the bed on.

The hallways grew quiet, though—in the distance—Christie could hear sobbing.

People have been lost.

In the battle, the war last night, when the power went out and they couldn't get it on again.

People have died.

And though the idea of sleeping seemed impossible—not with the swirl of thoughts she had—her fatigue was greater.

And amazingly she could close her eyes.

Closed tight, and before she knew it, time went by as if it didn't exist.

*

And then it was morning. The kids still asleep.

Karen came in the room, her face locked into a stony expression, her eyes looking everywhere but at Christie.

She didn't question that the kids were here. Didn't say anything at all at first, as if the terrible events of last night hadn't happened at all.

But then she must have felt Christie looking at her, and finally the woman let her eyes trail up and meet Christie's.

"Karen," Christie said.

Thinking, *What else can I say? What happened last night? Did we lose people?*

How many?

We lost…

Is it true, she wondered, *are we now a* we?

But Karen thankfully spoke, the words sounding normal. Life in this world going on.

"Will be a little late for any food. After last night…"

The nurse looked at Simon, the rifle at his feet. It seemed as if she might say something then, but instead turned back to Christie's bed.

"Going to be a while before the doc gets in. I mean, he—"

She stopped, the words unable to keep coming.

"I know," said Christie.

Then, "I'm doing much better. Think I'm good with a cane."

A nod. As if the state of Christie's recovery didn't matter much.

And Christie had to agree. Compared it all the bodies outside.

Because she knew that—out in the lot, near the fence, *on* the fence—there had to be the corpses of so many Can Heads.

Thank God it's so cold.

Then, as soon as she had that thought, *God? Did I really in my mind* thank *God?*

For this world?

For my son being able to get a gun and use it?

For this universe twisted into something primal, prehistoric, human against human. Except everyone knew all too well they weren't human?

And the outcome of that war?

Far from certain.

"Okay," Karen said, "You just rest here. Until he comes. It's a mess out there..."

Christie nodded.

She'd wait. To talk to the doctor. But first, she knew she'd have to talk to her kids.

*

Kate awoke first, turning in the bed, having slept through the lights coming on, the chat with Karen—some amazing ability to block all that out.

She looked at her mother, then around the room, as if not understanding how she got here.

She reached for Christie's hand and held it.

"Morning," Christie whispered.

Then, as if checking she hadn't misplaced something, Kate raised her head a bit, spotted Simon on the chair, then lay back again.

"You okay?" Christie said.

A nod.

As if anyone could be okay after a night like that.

A sound from the chair. Simon turning over, and then his eyes opening.

"Hey," Christie said.

And not a moment after seeing her, Christie watched as Simon's eyes trailed down to the floor, down to the gun.

He took a breath.

And then, as if they had planned this next move, Kate released her hand and slid off the bed.

Simon released the recliner so it was upright, and then he too stood up.

"May not be any food for a while," she said.

Christie almost added, *after last night.*

But that wasn't necessary. They had been in it.

Seen it.

Kate moved around the bed so she came to stand beside her brother. Once—not that long ago—it seemed like all they did was bicker.

Not anymore.

Christie hoped for the day where they'd do that again: whine, complain… fight over such unimportant things.

And without any sign that they had in fact worked this out, Kate took the lead.

"Mom, we have to do something."

A nod from Simon—totally on board.

And even Christie was surprised by her own answer—the realization happening just then.

"I know…"

Dr. Martin walked into the room and Christie could see the fatigue in his eyes. And blood spatters on his white jacket, as if bit by bit, the civilized life of this place, this hospital, was slipping away from him.

"You three…" he said, his voice phlegmy, sounding worn down by the events of the night, "…you okay?"

Christie nodded.

It took a minute for him to look up and take in the fact that Christie sat, fully upright, in the bed. Simon standing by the bed, Kate by his side.

He stopped.

From what little she knew of him, the doctor seemed perceptive.

After last night, he knows something is up.

Christie—having rehearsed it in her head—didn't waste any time getting to the point. "Doctor, we have to leave."

He shook his head. "Y-you're not ready. Still need days."

And now she did exactly as she planned.

Christie slid out of the bed, Simon moving to the side to make room for her as she swung her legs over, and out.

Then slowly to the floor.

Kate handed her the cane, and Christie stood up. As if she was proving something to the doctor.

"No, I'm not ready, Doctor. Could use—what—weeks recuperating? But after last night, we don't have weeks."

Then unexpected—but powerfully touching—Kate's voice, strong, steady.

Her daughter's new voice. "We need to leave here."

For a moment, no one said anything, but when she glanced at Simon, she thought he'd add his words as well.

But instead, her son stood there as the three of them gave the doctor some time to respond.

"Okay. Last night. It was…" The doctor looked away, eyes staring into some unfathomable distance. What had he done to help people?

What had he seen?

How many had they lost?

Then, as if returning from a journey, he came back to Christie, but now also looking to Kate, Simon. Taking note that they were all together. "But how will you drive?"

"I can do it," Kate said. "I got us here."

Then Simon spoke.

Sweet, beautiful Simon.

"She was good. She can drive."

A nod.

Then, "We'll take our chances," Christie said. "Better than staying here, waiting for the next attack, the next failure."

And now the doctor walked over to the bed as if this discussion had made him so tired, and he sat on the edge of the bed.

"Okay. You'll leave… I'll do what I can to help."

"We'll need our car. The guns we brought. Any food you can spare."

He shook his head. "That… will be hard. You've seen the people out there. No way they'd give you anything like that."

Then he took a breath. "But I'll try to get something for you. But it won't be much, won't last long."

"And... some antibiotics? I mean, I'm mending well."

His eyes locked on hers. "We have so little. And how much will we need in the days to come? I dunno."

"Whatever you can," Christie said.

Finally the doctor stood up. "When will you do this?"

Christie looked from Simon to Kate, then back to him. "As soon as we can. An hour... bit more if necessary."

A nod.

"Okay. I'll talk to the people outside. They won't like it. Giving you the guns, the ammo..."

"They're ours," Simon said.

The doctor smiled at that. "Yes, they are. Simon. Still—trust me—it won't be that easy. Your car has the gas your came with. Can't give you any more."

"That's okay" Christie said, not at all sure it was okay at all.

"Right, then. Let me tell them. You can get ready. Then I'll come back when it's all set, okay?"

He started for the door out of the room then—just at the doorway—stopped and turned.

"One more thing. When you leave, best do it quickly. People these days... can change their minds."

"We'll just go," Christie said.

"Yes. Good."

And then, moving slowly, as if feeling the burden of this place, the doctor walked out of the room, leaving them alone.

two

The Road Ahead

13
Survival

After struggling to get dressed, Christie felt a jab of panic.

Is this insane? she thought.

When simply walking, getting dressed, doing just about anything seemed so difficult.

But then she only had to look at her kids standing by the window, ready, waiting.

The looks on their faces saying that whatever they went through last night, they would not go through again.

And I won't let them go through that again.

Then they waited for the doctor to return, and that waiting itself felt terrible, as if something might happen that might stop them.

But finally he came in, his face grim as Karen followed close behind.

The doctor carried a canvas satchel, while the nurse had a powder blue plastic bag with the hospital's name—something patients could use to take personal things home with them.

The nurse shut the door.

"Okay," the doctor said. "I have your weapons." He looked at his nurse. "Wasn't easy. They weren't... happy."

Kate walked over and took the canvas bag, placed it on the bed, and began digging through it. "The bullets?" she asked.

"What?" Christie said, using her cane to walk over to the open bag.

Her daughter turned to the doctor. "We had a whole lot more than what's here."

The doctor nodded. "They said they ran through so much last night. That's all they could spare."

By now Simon had also walked over. "It's all right," he said.

Christie saw him look right at Kate. "We should just *go*."

And Christie thought she could guess what Simon was feeling.

Such a terrible, heavy thought for a boy not yet a teenager to carry.

That thought: *We'd better get out of here—now.*

And thankfully Kate picked up on it, nodded.

Karen came over with the blue bag. "Christie, I've put some food in here. And grabbed some of these."

She gave her the bag and then slipped a prescription bottle into her other hand.

"Antibiotics. Twice a day," Dr. Martin said. "Until you run out. A few painkillers. Wish I could spare more. I'm afraid… they watch the meds as well."

Christie nodded.

"Thank you. Both of you."

"There's also sandwiches in there, bottles of water."

A nod from Christie, this plan seeming more mad by the moment, and at the same time, more inevitable, more urgent.

It's time to leave.

But with a look at the closed door, she realized that the doctor had something else to say.

And Christie, flanked by her two kids, sat back down on the hospital bed.

"Look—it's hard to say where one should go these days," the doctor said. "North, south, east, west? Cities, open country? Small towns? The information we get… always so mixed. Cities look like war zones. Some small towns completely abandoned."

"And we know less every day," Karen added, shaking her head.

"But there was one thing I wanted to tell you. Not sure it's a good idea, that it makes any sense for you."

"You've been so helpful, doctor," Christie said. "And you, Karen."

"Wish I could do more. But here's the thing. A few weeks back, there were even more people here. And another doctor."

Christie nodded, listening, unable to guess where this was heading.

"Dr. Sam Collier. He had worked in Washington, studying this thing. But when it all took a turn for the worse, he came back here, to his home town."

"And he left?"

"Yes. He said, well much as you do, that this place could turn into a trap. People were divided. There were fights…"

Christie grabbed Kate, then Simon's hand.

No secrets anymore, she thought. *The kids deserve to hear everything, know everything.*

"He and a lot of others left. Dead of night. Wanted me to go, but, well, all these people staying… I couldn't abandon them."

"So, I stayed too," Karen said.

"Where did they go?" Christie said.

"He had heard things. About people leaving the cities. To a place that could be safer, talk of food stockpiled from the summer. A place where they had still been able to have fields that produced crops. God, a place where there was even livestock."

The doctor took a breath.

"More importantly, a place that could be defended."

Then it slowly dawned on Christie why he was telling her this.

It was a bit of hope.

About something out there.

"He had a name, a location. Halfway between the Ausable River and Thunder Bay."

Christie shook her head. "Where's that?"

"Sorry. So far away. Thought he was crazy. Northern Michigan.

Hunting country. Once. They would travel as a caravan."

He took a breath. "Did they ever get there? Who knows…"

Christie nodded.

"They've been gone for weeks. Anything could have happened to them. And, God, so far away."

He looked right at her then. "But rather than you just… heading out there."

Christie nodded again.

That thought—leaving for who knows where—put an icy pit in her stomach.

Thinking that leaving here might be even more dangerous than staying.

"I can show you the area they were heading to… trying to get to… Sam was a smart man. If you find them, well, it might be 'hope.'"

Hope? Christie thought.

A chance at survival?

Because that's what all this is about.

The doctor pulled a spiral book from the blue bag on the bed.

"Hard to believe," he laughed. "A road atlas. The entire US of A. So 'old-school.' Had this in my trunk. We all got so used to relying on our phones for everything."

He handed it to Christie.

"Rand McNally," she said, reading.

The doctor reached over and flipped the over-sized book open. "Here's the spot. A few miles from Hubbard Lake. Other CDC scientists had gone there after Washington was overrun. You see… not easy to get to, even for Can Heads."

Christie could see where Dr. Martin had circled areas.

"Sam… the people who left… they could end up there. If they made it. But you see, it's something, isn't it? A destination?"

Christie nodded.

"Michigan," she said. "So far." Then, "Thank you."

"Not much help, I know," the doctor said. "And I haven't

marked their route. They weren't sure how'd they go, where it was safe, where it wasn't. And what was safe then… may be dangerous now. Best use your instincts, ask people along the way. If you can trust them."

He took a breath, as if the idea of what Christie and her kids were about to do seemed overwhelming.

"As to gas, food…"

Two more thoughts that nearly paralyzed Christie.

"We'll manage," she said. Not sure at all about that.

Another squeeze of her kids' hands.

And then it was time.

She stood up.

"Somehow…" A look at Kate, Simon. "We've been through a lot."

Then with as much confidence as she could project, "We'll be okay."

The doctor nodded.

"Best go, then."

He walked over to the door. But, just before turning the knob, and getting ready to walk with them out to the main door—that entrance now looking as if it had been bombed—he looked at Kate.

"And you, Miss Kate. Drive slowly, carefully. Till your mom can take over."

He smiled.

And Christie knew that no matter what lay ahead, she'd miss this man, his help, his humanity.

Then they all walked out to the hallway, and the way out of the hospital.

14
Escape

Kate knew that backing up and turning around would be tricky for her, especially as she felt the eyes of people at the doorway locked on her.

There had been no one wishing them "good luck," just a silent line of people glaring at them as they walked out.

"Steady, Kate," she heard her mother say.

And while driving here, running away from the Mountain Inn hadn't seemed hard, driving in the night, everyone so scared, her mother hardly able to walk now...

This... was different.

Everyone watching while we sneak away.

Bright sunshine hit the windshield, the eyes of the people on her as if waiting for her to hit something, to do something that would make them rush over, stop them.

Take our guns, take the little food they were given, take the car...

Steady, she thought.

Her hands grabbed the steering wheel as if it might fly out of hands.

Kate looked up to the rearview mirror. She knew that kids near her age took weeks, even months... learning how to do things like this.

Her mother had turned around to look at the fence just behind them.

"Okay. Close enough," her mom said.

Kate took her foot off the gas pedal and—too quickly—braked.

Even at such a slow speed, the sharp braking made the car rock.

Then her mother turned and looked right at her.

"Now, just turn the wheel *before* you move. Way to the right. Might be enough room for you to pull out, pull away. If not—"

"I know…" Kate said, hearing how her voice sounded strange, strained, as if her mother's words were annoying her. "…I might have to back up again."

With all those eyes on her.

She turned the wheel as hard as she could. And when it wouldn't go anymore to the right, she took a breath. Foot on the brake, and now with what she hoped was the gentlest of touches, just pressing lightly, the car moved forward, with both her and her mother looking to see if they would clear the building, then the way out, off the hospital grounds, finally clear.

"Think you're okay, Kate," her mom said.

But to Kate… it looked like the left front corner of this car would hit the brick wall of the hospital building.

She shook her head. "It's going to *hit*, Mom. I better back up. I…"

Then her mother reached over and put a hand on Kate's left hand, locked on the steering wheel.

"You're okay. It's hard to gauge distance, things that come with practice. You'll clear it."

And then, as if her mother's words made it true, she kept applying the smallest amount of gas, the car lumbering into its turn.

Where—amazingly—it did clear the building.

Straighten out, she told herself.

Her mother pulled her hand away, Kate again in control.

She eased the car to the gate, now fully up and electrified again.

On the side: piles of Can Head bodies that had been cleared from the entrance, their bodies, a grisly heap of blood and bone.

Like something from a blender, she thought.

She forced herself to focus on looking straight ahead.

Until they reached the gate. Another shift from the accelerator to the brake.

The gate not moving, not opening.

"Come on, come on," she heard her mother say.

Kate was tempted to look back at the hospital entrance, a place where Can Head bodies mixed with the people who fought last night and didn't make it.

From the back, she heard Simon's voice.

"Mom, they're not going to let us out."

Kate wanted to tell Simon, *Shut up. Just shut up. They have to let us out; they will let us out. Please…*

Silence. Then over the rumble of the car's engine, the whirring sound of a motor, and the gate slowly grinding opening.

That opening gate, such a welcome sight when they came to the hospital only days ago.

Now, the one thing between them and escape.

Because that's what this was Kate knew—an escape.

The only question, *What are we escaping to?*

And when the gate was fully open, Kate looked at her mother. A nod.

And filling her lungs with air, the tension unbearable, she gave enough gas to the car so that it lumbered out of the parking area, through the gate that she knew would quickly—and forever—close behind them.

Out to the road.

To whatever lay ahead.

Whatever lay ahead, she thought. *And what would that be?*

But for now, she concentrated on the task at hand, the now so-much-simpler task of driving the car slowly on the road, no sharp turns needed, nice and steady.

Never relaxing, hands still locked on, while nobody said anything.

Simon pressed the button to lower his window.

The car heater seemed to blast all its musty hot air right at him.

But as soon as he did, his mother turned back to him.

"Simon... best keep the window up."

"It's so *hot,* Mom. I can't even breathe."

As soon as he said the words he felt guilty.

He constantly told himself, *got to be nice to Mom. After everything that's happened to her.*

And Kate too.

Kate! She had saved him.

He nodded. "Okay."

"I'll turn down the heat," his mom said.

And Simon hit the button and the back window went up.

And when his mother turned back to the windshield, he looked out at this town they were driving through.

Thinking, *Is everyone gone? Everyone that was left either inside that hospital place, all those grim-faced people? And the others turned into Can heads? I hate Can heads.*

He realized something then. That the hate he felt was something so strong, so powerful... that just having that thought, he felt his body tense, fists balled.

Thinking... how much he wanted to shoot them.

After all they'd done to him. His dad, gone; his family running away.

And finally what was the most terrible thought.

There was a time when Can Heads didn't exist. And that time was gone, gone forever.

And then a question that he doubted he could tell anyone, certainly not his mom, not his sister: *Was this to be his life now? All the years ahead. This?*

He looked at the handgun on the seat beside him.

His mom no longer asked for the guns, the bullets to be put away.

Not anymore.

Simon knowing that he could never be far from his gun.

And then as he went back to looking at the street outside, passing one house that looked in perfect shape, then another burned, a blackened wreck after some crazy attack.

That the three of them in this car were—for now—all they had. All that was left of their family.

His whole world was in this beat-up car that wasn't even theirs.

The houses flew by outside, and trashed, burned out cars as well, while Simon kept thinking these things.

15
Detour

Christie looked at the map on her lap while Kate drove quietly. She could feel her daughter's confidence growing.

Now in the quiet, she studied the possibilities ahead, wondering...

What are we doing?

What are we going to do?

The Pennsylvania border was ahead, leaving New Jersey behind. Leaving the great cluster of cities of the Northeast. But ahead were big cities as well—Scranton, Allentown—all places she felt they had to avoid, any one of them a trap.

And the roads as well. The giant highways like 80 and 78 couldn't be trusted.

But—now on Route 212—they were coming up to a town with a peaceful name: Clear Lake.

And Christie couldn't help but look down at the gas gauge. Already well below one-quarter. Both her kids had eaten one of the sandwiches that Karen had given them.

She had decided not to eat hers.

Best to be safe, she thought.

Remembering so many books and films she had read about survival. When survival became an issue, rationing had to be done.

She didn't stop the kids from eating theirs. Kate holding the wheel with one hand, Simon making his dry tasteless sandwich disappear even after saying, "*I hate this stuff.*"

Back to the map. The town just ahead.

When they saw a roadblock.

Sure. Not unexpected.

Men outside, standing around, a few smoking. Guns on their arms.

"Gotta slow down here, Kate."

A nod from her daughter as she followed those instructions.

For a moment, with their car stopped right at their barricade, nothing happened.

Then one of the men climbed over the makeshift wall of lumber, old furniture, chunks of metal, and came around to the car.

The man walked slowly, cautiously, as if anything could happen.

And Christie had to think, *Has it only taken these months for everything to get to this?*

Barricades? Guarded roads? Men with guns everywhere?

And she felt something else at that moment as well.

This idea: *Maybe these men aren't just here to* protect *their small town with the bucolic-sounding name of Clear Lake, PA.*

Maybe there were other things that they were here for.

He started to walk around to the driver side window, but Christie hit the button on hers.

"Hi. Sir…"

The word sounding ridiculous.

Sir.

"You can talk to me," Christie said from the passenger seat. "Maybe you can help…"

The man stopped, looked at Kate, a teenage girl behind the wheel, then to Christie in the front passenger seat. He looked back at his fellow guards at the barricade.

Then he came around to Christie's window.

"Hi," she began again. "We're heading west, toward…"

She named a city at the other end of the state, picked randomly in those moments the man ambled over "…Erie. Hoping to cut through here."

The man shook his head.

"Erie, hmm? Well, don't think you're going there."

Christie forced a smile. "Um… is there a problem?"

The man leaned down, now taking in Simon sitting in the back. His eyes looking tired, milky. Too little sleep, too much booze?

Too much… something?

"No one goes through *here*."

She turned to Kate. Sitting here, they were just burning gas.

"Kate, shut the car off."

"Look, lady," the man said raising his voice, "I told you, you can't go through here, so you'll have to back up, and turn the hell around."

Christie nodded quickly.

"Okay, I got it. No cut through. But can you tell me the best way west from here? I see there's a route 61, and—"

"Don't know about any of those other damn roads. The Interstate is ahead… if you can get to it."

Christie shook her head. "No, we're trying to stay off the big highways."

The man grinned as if that idea was funny. "Good thinking right there, lady. Don't want to get caught… on a long empty stretch of highway."

Christie knew from few radio newscasts they'd picked up back at the Mountain Inn that the Highway Patrol had long abandoned the big highways, now forced back to deal with towns and cities overwhelmed with Can Heads.

And then… dealing with those others…

Human as she was.

But in some way, now even more monstrous, more dangerous. Driven by hunger, they captured people.

Like herds. Kept them alive.

Until they were needed.

In the rearview mirror, she saw Simon's eyes locked on hers.

She knew that his hand would be on his gun.

What a strange world to be a young boy in.

"You can't tell me a good way—?"

A laugh. "Good way? You fu—um, serious—lady? Good way… what? To live? Find food? To get from here to wherever the hell it is you are going?"

He stood there, glaring at her as if it was somehow all her fault.

He spat at the ground. "No. I. *Can't*. Guess all the 'good ways' are all gone."

Christie nodded, then to Kate.

This was turning bad. Best they just leave.

"Kate, start the car. We've got to turn around."

Having managed her tricky three-point turn back at the hospital, Christie hoped Kate didn't take too long with this maneuverer.

Not with this man here, growing angrier by the minute.

And when she looked back, she saw one of the other men step around the barricade and also start walking over.

"Kate…"

Kate hadn't turned the key enough to start the ignition, but now, with another twist, the engine started up.

Thank God for that, she thought.

Then, to the man, "We're leaving." But she heard another voice, a man yelling from the barricade.

"Tim, tell those folks to hang on."

The man by the car—this Tim—stood up, backing away from the open window, which Christie quickly shut.

She didn't have to tell Kate anything more.

They had seen enough together to know when something was happening, and it wasn't good.

Kate put the car into reverse, and twisted her head around as she gunned the car backwards, leaving the two men behind.

So easy, Christie knew, for them to raise their weapons and try to stop them.

After all, she thought, *we have guns, we have a goddamn car. They might even think we have food.*

Then Kate hit the brakes as she came abreast a narrow two-lane road that veered left, away from the barricade, away from the town of Clear Lake.

With a jerky pull on the shifter, Kate put the transmission in drive and gunned the car forward, wheels squealing, dust flying, leaving the men, the town, and their makeshift barricade behind.

*

"Mom, where are we going? Where am I driving to?"

Kate looked over at her, the old road atlas open on her lap.

And she had to think, *How long would it take to drive to—God— Michigan? Nine… ten hours? More?* Which meant days of driving.

And that was on highways.

But wandering around like this, using side roads, old routes even before the interstates and throughways?

Probably getting lost.

She turned to her daughter. "Not sure, Kate. But this road circles around that town. We can get back on that bigger road."

Then, "You okay? You've been driving a while."

With her hands locked on the steering wheel, Kate looked anything but okay.

"I'm fine, Mom. Just want to know what we're doing, where we're going."

Christie nodded.

Of course.

Wishing she had something better to stay, wondering if leaving the hospital had—in the end—been a bad idea.

She turned back to Simon.

'And you, mister? You all right?"

Keeping it light.

Simon nodded. Christie gave him a big smile, hoping that would reassure her son, that somehow he might summon a smile to send back.

But only a nod, his gaze turning back to the window. Who knew what thoughts were running through his head?

Then, "Mom. Something ahead."

Christie felt Kate slow the car.

16
Going Shopping

Christie saw a sign on the side of the road: WELCOME TO THE HAMLET OF STORMVILLE.

And below the welcome, a smaller welcome sign from a Unitarian church.

Another town, she thought.

But the map didn't show it.

She brought the road atlas closer, studying the web of roads, and then she saw a small dot, miles still away from any major road, and the letters—a very small *S'ville.*

Kate slowed some more, then stopped.

She turned to Christie. "This okay? I mean, okay for us to drive through?"

But Christie had another idea. She didn't know how big this Stormville was, but from the size of its name and dot on the map, pretty damn small.

And looking ahead, she saw no movement.

The Wild West, she thought. *A ghost town.*

Their gas was low. The sandwiches gone. A few hours till dark.

"Okay. How about you drive in slowly? Let's just take a look. See what's going on here."

"I don't like it," Simon said.

Christie was reminded that she had said to the two of them,

We're together. Things will be decided together.

She turned back to her son. "Just a look, Simon. Okay? We don't like what we see, we just keep going?"

No need to tell him how low the gas was getting.

He nodded. Agreement.

What a world three of us live in.

"Okay," she said to Kate.

The car started moving again.

The town—what there was of it—looked deserted.

A tiny post office sat next to a storefront that proclaimed it to be the Stormville Public Library.

Even the church looked miniature.

A few cars dotted the street, most looking undamaged, but farther into the two-street-long town, she saw one blackened wreck that looked as if it had been used for a bonfire.

And a small hardware store also showed signs of a major fire, all glass smashed, the shelves empty.

But diagonally across from that store... a small grocery store.

The Village Market.

Christie had hoped to spot a gas station, but she guessed people had to travel farther in either direction for that.

"Hang on, Kate."

Her daughter's foot came off the accelerator.

No one around.

This town, like so many in the past few months, probably abandoned, people fleeing toward some mythical safe place.

Just like us.

"What?" Kate said, and Christie heard a strain in her voice.

Could their nerves be pulled any tighter?

She made a note that when the time was right, somehow they had to find a way to just *be* together, not running not shooting, a few moments to be a family.

"That market—"

Simon pointed out the obvious.

"Mom, that will be *empty*. People would have taken everything. This whole place is empty."

A nod. Then, "Probably right, Simon. But…"

She didn't want to let him know how desperate she was beginning to feel.

"But a small store like that… maybe has some storerooms. People would have grabbed what they could off the shelves, but *maybe*—"

"I doubt that," Simon said.

And even she had to admit his questioning made more sense.

But what choice did they have? They could find water in the small lakes and ponds on the roads ahead.

But food?

She patted Kate's knee as she turned to Simon. Hoping that Kate would stand with her.

"Worth a look-see? Just a look? We can be quick."

"Mom, what about the gas?" Kate said.

Christie had hoped she wouldn't have noticed that. Or noticing it, kept quiet.

"Got an idea about that too. But first… the market. A look around. What do you say?"

No quick answer.

Then Simon nodded.

"Okay," Kate said. "I could use a break."

"And you thought driving would be fun," Christie said.

Kate smiled.

The smallest crack in the mood.

But enough. It was something.

"Let me park closer," she said to Christie.

And she eased the car right in front of the grocery store with its empty shelves.

Now for a plan.

She could—Christie thought—just run in, see if she could find anything left behind, leave the kids here.

But no.

She remembered what happened when they returned to their home on Staten Island, how the kids, left in the car, had been overwhelmed by Can Heads.

It may look quiet here, she thought.

Things could change quickly.

And with her bad leg, hobbling around the place, if she *did* find any food left behind, how could she carry it?

"Okay. We lock the car up, and all go in. Stick together, right?"

"Sure," Kate said, answering for both herself and her brother.

"And the guns—"

"We bring them," Simon said, as if that idea was about to be questioned.

"Yes. Of course. But safeties on. You know how… just like your father—"

She stopped.

Months later.

The mere mention of him… so devastating.

After that man… Their father had given his life to save them. Just thinking of him brought such terrible pain.

She looked away. Took a breath.

"Like your dad showed you. Safety first."

In this completely unsafe world.

"All set?"

Then, moving her wounded leg, feeling the wound pull, she popped open the door and stepped out into the chilly air.

Colder than she thought.

Were they up in some hills, mountains? Seemed so much colder than back at the hospital in New Jersey.

She pulled her collar tight around her neck.

"Button up, guys. Freezing here."

The kids flanked her as they entered the market, one glass door just a frame, the other smashed and hanging off its hinges as they climbed over and around them.

Still painful, but Christie also noticed this: the pain seemed better. The dressing, the antibiotics, doing their work.

Not wincing with every move she made.

Then, into the store, the empty shelves ghostly, signs still up announcing sales. To the left, what must have been a produce section.

A few rotten, decayed strands of something lay on the floor.

Long past fitting the definition of food.

To the right, a dairy section, equally barren.

Anything and everything that could be eaten, all gone.

If they were going to find anything, it wouldn't be here.

"Let's check the back. Places they might store stuff."

She led the way down an aisle where—amazingly—there were still some full shelves.

With dishwashing liquid. Sponges. Air freshener!

As if that part of the world—that part of life—was still normal.

People doing dishes, keeping things clean and fresh.

No.

Just that when you need to find things to eat, all that was useless.

They walked past a small gardening section. Some weed killer. Rolls of green garden hoses.

No seed though.

'Cause probably… if you're hungry enough…

"Mom, I don't think we'll find anything here," Simon said.

Which was exactly what Christie was beginning to think. Place picked clean. How could anything be overlooked?

"I know, Simon. But we're here. Let's look anyway."

More steps, her kids slowing so they matched her hobbling walk forward.

Until they hit the back of the tiny market.

The meat section.

Signs announcing *freshly ground beef.*

Ground beef? That would have disappeared even during the best of times over the past few years.

And like all the other counters, the white, smeared here and there with what looked like blood, all the refrigerated cases empty.

This was all beginning to feel so hopeless.

But then—at back—double swinging doors.

To the back room. Maybe to storage areas.

Maybe, maybe, maybe…

She looked at her kids. Their faces said that they didn't like this crawl through the barren store.

This had been a bad idea.

Still, she gave the door a push, So dark inside with no power, just a filmy light from grimy windows at the back.

Any flashlights in the store would have been long taken.

They had one in the car.

Didn't think to bring that, she thought. *Got to think of things more clearly.*

Can't make mistakes, miss things.

Her kids followed her inside.

17
A Surprise

"Hang on," Christie said. Though there were some filmy windows at the back of the storeroom, still the darkness here made it near impossible to see.

"Let's let our eyes adjust. Just a second," she said.

She didn't like it back here. The musty smell of the store's backroom, once filled with crates and cartons of goods to be brought outside to the gleaming store.

Now, as her eyes did in fact slowly adjust, she could see how empty the storage shelves were. On a few, she saw the ripped-open carcasses of the boxes that had been pillaged for anything edible they might hide.

Like a strange slaughterhouse, the ripped cardboard dotting the floor, the shelves.

"Nothing here," Simon said, disappointment in his voice.

Christie turned to him. "Doesn't appear that way. Sorry, kids."

And Kate, ever more aware of her mother it seemed to Christie, came over. "It's okay, Mom. Was worth a look."

She nodded.

But she also felt that desperation, that terrible thought, *What if we don't find food?*

Had I been foolish leaving the hospital?

Then another terrible thought, *Could we go back?*

But she doubted that even if she made that decision that they would welcome that back.

Some doors when they close… close forever.

Simon had walked away, running a hand along a shelf, knocking the splayed boxes off their perch to the ground below.

Until…

"Hey! Look at this. Over here."

Kate looked at Christie, and then staying with her, giving her mother a helpful arm, additional support beyond her cane, as they walked to the back.

"Bunch of empty boxes piled here. I kicked them away… and look."

Christie looked down to where Simon stood. And though so dark, she saw the outlines of *something*.

An opening.

And at the top, embedded in the panel, something you'd miss so easily if you weren't looking around carefully—a ring.

For pulling open a trapdoor.

"Simon. You found something."

Simon knelt down, and she watched him pry the ring up.

But it wouldn't move. Simon's smile vanished.

"Kate, can you try to help?"

Now both of her kids had their fingers trying to lock on the ring, but still it remained stuck, as if the ring wasn't designed to pop open at all.

"Need something to pry it open," Christie said. She looked around for a tool—probably unlikely to be found—or simply a sturdy piece of metal.

And always the idea that this was another pointless search.

Wondering how many dead ends she could take before she cracked, even as she knew she had to be strong for her family.

Then, off in a corner, she saw a twisted chunk of metal, maybe from a storm window frame that had broken, the jagged metal piece just left here.

Would it be strong enough?

She didn't wait for the kids to help her but walked as quickly as she could with her cane to the storeroom's back left corner, reached down and picked up the piece of metal.

As soon as she felt it, she knew that if the ring could be pried open, this metal rod could do it.

The metal hard, unyielding when she tried to make it bow.

Solid enough, she thought.

She hurried back to where her two kids still clawed at the ring.

"Try this," she said. "Wedge it under the ring." She handed Simon the bar.

Now she watched her kids work the bar back and forth, trying to get under the ring, make it open up.

Please, she thought. If the ring was that resistant, then people could easily have ignored it, even if they saw it.

And if it had been ignored, there could be something down there.

Back and forth, her kids worked with the metal piece... like a book she had read to them both centuries ago.

Two Little Miners.

Then, "Mom, Mom! It's moving," Simon said.

And with a click—one of the best sounds she had heard in her life—the ring popped up, as if getting it freed from its entrenched hole wasn't difficult at all.

"Okay," Christie said. "Put one tip of the bar into the ring, then bring the bar down to the floor, try to..."

She realized how hard it was to explain such a simple principle as using a bar as a lever.

But she could see—even in this darkness—that Simon understood what to do, and with Kate's help, now had the bar flush to the ground, then both of them pulling up on it, trying different angles.

When—the most amazing thing of all—the trap door began to open with another welcome sound, a loud creaking.

Until halfway up, it suddenly became easy for her kids to flip it fully open.

Exposing a dark basement.

And for a moment they all just stood around the gaping hole.

Christie leaned forward, peering down.

Kate confirmed the problem: "I can't see a thing."

But Simon, on his stomach on the floor, had leaned down with one arm, waving it back and forth.

"There are *stairs*," he said. "We can get down."

"But we can't see!" Kate said.

Christie made a decision. Fast, and one she questioned—for so many reasons as soon as she said it.

"Kate, run to the car, go get our flashlight. It's worth a shot. But be careful!"

It was getting dark, and though it would undoubtedly be safer if they all trudged back to the car at Christie's speed, the trapdoor was open, there was a ladder. Kate could just get the light, hurry back.

Kate looked at her mom as if recognizing the risk of what was being proposed.

Then a nod.

"Okay, Mom."

As if asking her to empty the dishwasher.

And then before Christie could change her mind, Kate ran out of the storeroom, her gun jutting out of the back of her belt.

No need for me to remind her to bring the gun, Christie thought.

Simon kept his head buried in the open hole.

"It stinks down here," he said, always one with the report for whatever unusual smells they ever encountered.

Something so funny about him.

Simon's nose reports!

And with seconds seeming like minutes, they waited for Kate to come back.

18
Down the Rabbit Hole

"Hang on tight, Simon. Take the steps slowly."

Kate held the flashlight above the opening, pointed down into the basement area. Now the rank smell from below filled the storeroom.

What would they find down there?

Simon faded into the shadows, the flashlight only making just the top of his head visible.

Christie watched him turn around.

"I can't see a thing!"

Then Kate turned to her. "Okay, Mom—going down,"

Christie nodded. She turned and looked at the window at the back. Already the patch of gloomy light that it admitted was dimming, the afternoon growing late, the late winter night ready to reclaim this hamlet.

And she thought: *We can't stay here too long. Not when it turns dark.*

She watched Kate jam the flashlight in her jeans pocket, good and deep. Then her daughter stretched down with one leg, feeling for that first step.

A nod indicating that she found it.

Christie watched Kate as she started down and, without the light pointing the way, it was as if she was stepping into utter darkness, the blackest of black holes.

Christie wanted to say to her: *Come back up. Forget this whole thing. There can't be anything down there.*

Or whatever is down there... has to be rotten, useless.

But in those seconds, her daughter's head disappeared into the darkness.

"Okay, Mom I'm down and—"

She turned on the flashlight, and in the glow Christie could now see Simon and Kate's faces.

"Good," she said. "Just a quick look, guys. Then we better go."

Christie looked over her shoulder.

She had been so absorbed looking down, peering into the hole that was swallowing her kids, that she became unaware of the store, the world outside.

For a few minutes, the universe had become just this opening to the basement the ladder down.

A glance behind her.

It was quiet out there.

She thought: *Everyone must have really left this village...*

A total ghost town.

And when she turned back to the opening, the light and her kids had moved away...

*

Until she heard their voices, suddenly... excited.

"Mom!"

Kate.

Then Simon— even louder. "Mom—we found something!"

So frustrating to hear their voices and not be able to see.

"What is it?"

She still couldn't see them, but she heard a ripping noise.

Cardboard being torn.

"Some boxes," Kate said. "Just a few and—"

Then Simon: "Wow!"

What is it?

And Christie only hoped that maybe—just maybe—they had found something good, something that could help...

Dare she think it?

"Cans of food!" Simon yelled.

"There's peas, Mom!" Kate added.

"And—what's this?—soup! Tomato soup."

"And chicken soup!"

How is that even possible? Christie wondered.

Those things had become so incredibly rare, with various food substitutes replacing so many things that had suddenly become like gold.

Unless... someone—the guy who ran the store—hid them away here, a little cache for when things turned bad.

Except—what happened to him?

Did people break in, storm the place, do something to the guy who owned this tiny market?

His secret dying with him.

And now—by some miracle—she... her kids... got it.

Christie tried to think...what to do, how to do it... though the excitement of the discovery felt overwhelming.

"Okay, Kate—how many boxes?"

She waited.

A bit of disappointment in her daughter's voice.

"Only four, Mom. A couple dozen cans in each, I guess."

Okay, she thought. *Not a lot. But enough for their journey. Certainly more real food than they had eaten in a long time.*

Then the next question: "Can you lift the boxes?"

Because what good would it do if they can't get them up and out? Have to tediously pass single cans up?

If I could get down there, maybe I could lift a box.

But were her kids strong enough?

She waited.

Then: "Mom—Simon and I can lift one up... I think we can get them up the ladder, one at a time."

"Great, Kate. Just have to get it close to me, then I can help pull it up."

Then, thinking ahead... *Out to the car, in the trunk, maybe with minutes left before night falls.*

"Just hurry," she said, then realizing that she shouldn't really rush them. "As much as you can, okay?"

"Okay, Mom. We're starting."

And Christie thought, as she heard the kids struggle with the box, *my wonderful strong kids.*

So good, so powerful.

And this: how the love she had for them was so overpowering.

She heard them start moving up the ladder.

*

They nearly let the first box slip from their fingers, such an awkward move going up together, the heavy box held tight.

Easy, Christie thought.

But keeping any words to herself.

Then, she saw Simon in the lead, coming up slowly, walking backward on the old wooden ladder, hands locked on one end of a box while below, Kate did the harder work of constantly pushing it up.

And soon as she could, Christie put her gun to the side, away from the hole and grabbed at the corners of the box, easing the weight off her daughter, then sliding the box to the floor of the storeroom.

Without a nod, Simon turned around and went back to his sister and the next box.

Christie feeling useless in the job the kids were doing.

Then another box appeared, Simon's arms outstretched. And when she looked at his grim face she could see what a massive effort this was for him.

She hurried to pull that box up.

Then—in minutes, time seeming to crawl a bit longer for each recovery, the third box.

Until that too had been slid out onto the stone storeroom floor—and only one left to go.

Christie's heart racing, lost to this moment that could mean life and death for them on the road.

Lost to only that thought…

When she became aware of something else.

Her mind pulled back, a strange feeling at the back of her neck. Hairs on end.

She heard a grunt.

A low, rumbling… *grunt.*

Somebody had entered the store, making a noise.

Another grunt, now closer.

Until, she had an awareness that felt ancient, making her kids, the boxes, the hole—all vanish.

No, not someone.

Some thing….

19
The Attack

Then she saw it.

A shape in the doorway to the back storeroom.

Impossible to make out.

So little light.

It paused there, and for a while Christie hoped it was just someone also looking for food, or even—God—a Can Head.

But then, she knew it wasn't.

The shape bobbed its massive head, with the only clear part visible, its eyes reflecting the dull glow from the scant light here.

The shape of the head—clearly the primal shape of bear.

Christie felt frozen, more than she had in any moment since her nightmare began months ago.

She looked left. Her gun placed carefully on the floor, a yard away. Close. But still feet away.

Her kids' guns—even farther away.

"Mom, we're almost there," Simon bellowed.

The bear raised its head at the sound, a big snort, as if sniffing at the words, the scent.

Then a deeper growl.

And Christie had this devastating thought, *Everyone's hungry. There's so little food these days, and, and…*

What would a hungry bear do?

Then, with her still being frozen, the bear took a quick hop. Not a cautious step, but a sudden gamboling lope that closed the distance between them by half.

"Mom, come on, give us a hand!"

She wanted to tell her son to be quiet. But what would the bear do if she said anything, made any noise?

She had read of people having bear encounters, as close as New Jersey. Close calls, while people put out the garbage, or opened a backdoor on a chilly night and something stood there, *waiting.*

She tried to remember what those articles—always seeming so crazy, so unbelievable—said about what to do.

What to do.

And outside of a few things she remembered... like bears really have no interest in you, and, and... always back up slowly if you see one, she drew a blank.

Should she look at those eyes, or was that bad?

Should she make noise or stay stock still?

Should I make a quick stretch for the gun?

It wasn't that far away.

Could she get it, get the goddamned safety off, and fire... before the bear got to her?

The animal didn't seem that big. Maybe not full grown.

The bear tilted his head.

Now, after that bouncy jump in her direction, walking down an aisle toward her, it seemed slow, steady... cautious.

A bear hungry enough to—what?—wake up from some winter sleep, and go hunting?

No, she thought.

Not this.

Not after all they have survived.

"Mom!"

And now the bear was close enough that it reacted to her son's voice.

This time—the growl was big, deep, throaty, and the bear close enough that she could see in its open black maw, the canine teeth catching the light.

She remembered something else from all those stories, stories that seemed that they came from another planet.

Bears are fast.

Can't outrun them. Can't out-climb them.

"Simon," she said, had to say.

Then, "*Don't* come out. Go back down, Simon. *Now.*"

She kept her voice steady, thinking that might not prompt the bear to do anything quick.

To do whatever its primal brain was telling it.

With the bear closer, her gun seemed even farther away, the distance of the two about the same.

But when she spoke, she immediately realized that she shouldn't have said anything, because two terrible things happened.

And for a moment, all Christie could do was watch.

First, Simon again.

So loudly.

"Mom, we did it *ourselves.*"

And without turning around, not taking her eyes off the black bear, Christie knew her son had come out of the dark hole, still unaware of this danger.

But then, the bear reared up on two legs, its paws outstretched in a bow as if it could encircle whatever was in front of it, then dig in with giant claws.

And it roared—crazed, angry—or maybe excited that now there were two people here.

Christie wanted to tell Simon to turn around, go back down, jump the hell down if he had to.

But now, with the quickest of sideways glances, she saw her son had turned into a statue, standing so still as this lumbering beast—taller than her now, no cub, jaw opening and shutting again and again, as if anticipation—started right for her son.

And Christie thought, *No.*

The thought focusing her entire body in service to one goal.

To race to the gun while the bear—distracted, focused, moving—might not turn to her as she bolted for her gun.

And as she did, she saw Simon back away, then move fast, but still no challenger for the lightning-quick bear who was ready to pin him to the ground in seconds.

But Christie—having fired her gun some many times, so much that it had become an extension of her own body—grabbed it off the floor, flicked the safety.

And with barely any time to aim, fired into darkness, at the black shape below the one window at the back of the storeroom.

She couldn't see her son.

So—even as she pulled the trigger once, then again, then again—the shots thunderously loud in here—she couldn't be sure that her sweet, brave boy wasn't in the line of fire.

She was about to fire again, when she realized that at the back wall of the storeroom, everything had turned still.

Kate had crawled out of the hole, head snapping from Christie then back to the wall, to the bear.

Then Kate—somehow able to move, somehow able to act—ran over and pulled her brother from that corner where wall met floor.

Christie could barely watch.

The bear's left paw lay on her son as Kate tugged and pulled.

Then, suddenly alert, Christie ran over and helped.

To see: her son breathing, his eyes wide. His face dotted with blood.

The bear's blood.

Together, she and Kate encircled him, holding him tight as could be.

And with the dead bear at their feet, they stayed that way for moments, her breathing returning to normal, as if they were all breathing with one set of lungs.

Christie thought, *how terrifying for Simon?*

How will we ever go on, how can we—

But when he spoke, she remembered that her son had *changed*. After everything they had experienced, everything he had done, her son had shown himself resilient, strong, and brave.

And his first words now echoed that.

"Mom, that was great shooting!"

Another squeeze from Christie.

Kate looked at her, dumbfounded as well, but said nothing.

"You-you okay?" Christie asked.

"Yeah, I mean, I didn't even know what was happening until it knocked me down. Hit my head against the wall…"

He rubbed his head.

And Christie thought, after all this, she'd take a bump, a bruise on her son's head.

Easily.

20
Night

Christie watched her kids carry the boxes to the car outside, ignoring the giant dead animal in the corner looking like a prop from a movie.

Simon, amazingly, seemed unfazed by what happened.

As for me, Christie thought, *it's all I can do to stop shaking.*

But she also thought, not for the first time, that she needed to be as strong as they were.

And when the boxes were in the trunk, Kate turned to her. "Anything else?"

And there was. Something Christy thought they needed... not for tonight, but tomorrow.

"Yes. Let's take a garden hose."

Kate look confused. "Really? What for?"

Christie looked around.

The streets dark now. A few lights were on, so some of this "hamlet" was still getting electricity. But she also saw that most of the lights were out.

With most of the stores and shops burned out, electricity didn't matter.

"Some of these cars here, the ones that aren't wrecks... they may have gas in them. We can use the hose as siphon, get that gas out."

"And you know how to do that?" Simon asked.

Christie smiled at that. "Sure. I know *how* to siphon. But no, Simon, I've never siphoned gas out of gas tank. Anyway, we can try it in the morning."

"I'll get one," her son said.

And in that moment when they were alone, Kate asked, "Mom, what are we going to do tonight?"

That was a question Christie had asked herself.

Can't go driving in the night; Kate has to be wiped anyway.

So what to do?

And Christie said: "I think... we can drive around. Look for a house, some place intact. With lights. We get in, stay there for the night."

In the reflected glow of the nearest streetlight, Kate's face didn't seem so sure. But after a moment's hesitation, she nodded.

Then Simon came running back with a big coil of green hose.

"Got it!" he said.

And they were ready to go.

As Kate took the car slowly up and down the streets of the hamlet, Christie looked at the houses.

Most of the ones they passed were dark. They could still have power, but then, even if they were abandoned, there should be a light on somewhere.

Other houses were ruins, as if they had been bombed decades ago and were now nothing but a collapsed roof, with black, charred timbers jutting up to the darkening sky.

What happened here? she wondered.

It looked as if a battle had taken place. And then a thought that made her stomach tight.

Had it been a war between people and Can Heads?

Or...

Or...

The people against themselves as well.

When panic set in, when food got low, when neighbor turned

against neighbor.

The story seemed written in the ruined homes.

"Mom, seeing anything?" Kate said.

Though the hamlet was small, Kate drove slowly, and Christie could hear the fatigue in her daughter's voice.

Once they passed a house that had a single light bulb on at the doorway.

But that light revealed the smashed picture windows, and Christie could make out burned out holes on the roof.

This hunt—prowling up and down the residential streets of the town, hitting cul de sacs, turning around—seemed hopeless.

One good thing: They had seen no Can Heads.

Maybe they too had left when everyone else did.

When your food supply moves... you move with it.

Like a wolf pack.

And she remembered something Jack had said so many months before, the night the Paterville Camp had been attacked, when the Can Heads broke in.

These Can Heads seemed to hunt in a pack.

Predators working together.

And Jack, having dealt with them for so long in New York, said that was new.

And what would a wolf pack do but follow the fleeing, terrified herd of humans, maybe pick them off one by one?

If that was true—and she felt guilty at thinking this—that could be her family's good luck. This small village and its surrounding woods and fields could be clear.

They came to yet another small cul-de-sac.

Three houses around a small circle where people probably once let their kids bike safely, the dead end keeping cars away.

Two of the houses on the circle were dark; Christie easily spotted the damage: blown-in windows, smashed doorways, charred walls.

But the third... at the top of the circle.

A light on at the door. Then, an interior light, maybe from a kitchen.

"Hang on," she said to Kate.

Kate slowed, a bit less jerkily now as she slowly became used to driving.

"Is that one okay, Mom?" Kate said.

"Not sure."

Christie kept looking at it, the bushes outside dappled with snow, clumps of dirty snow on the lawn.

But the windows looked intact. The door, not broken in.

Then, "May just be all right, Kate. Let's take a look. Pull up, into the driveway. Is…"

She turned back to her son. But Simon was asleep, flat on the back seat.

He may have acted like being pounced on by a black bear was "no big thing."

But there he was, asleep, tuned out.

Coping, she thought.

"Okay," Kate said.

And she slowly pulled closer to the house, then up the slanted driveway that would put the car only feet from the doorway.

Kate stopped the car.

Christie took a breath.

Time to take a look…

21
The House

Christie let Kate and Simon stay in the car, engine off, doors locked, while she went to the front door.

Locked, of course.

Which was a good thing. The door locked... might mean that someone could still be living here.

On that off chance—such a weird idea—she pressed the buzzer, which worked. She heard the near-absurd sound of deep chimes for the doorbell, as if Big Ben was tolling inside.

She waited, giving her kids a look, a smile. Then she rapped hard on the door.

Then again.

And the idea that someone was still here faded.

The house had been—for some unknown reason—spared.

But like the rest of the battle scene that was this town, it was abandoned.

Now, she thought, *how to get in?*

Until she felt a tap behind her.

She gasped, her nerves compete on edge.

To see Kate.

"Mom, can I help?"

Christie shook her head. "No. You should stay in the car, with your brother, and..."

Then, standing in the small pool of light made the doorway light, she nodded.

We're together, she reminded herself.

"Okay. It's locked. I'm guessing any back door will be as well."

"So how do we get in?"

"We could... well, I saw it done on TV... break the glass, unlock the door from the inside."

But Kate looked at the nearest window.

"Pretty cold, Mom. We'd have a hole in the window."

Right, Christie thought.

She wanted to find a place that was *intact*. Maybe not a good idea to start putting holes in it.

"Right."

She bent down and looked at the lock. "I saw your dad do something once. We came in our back door, didn't have a key. He slipped in a credit card..."

Credit card, she thought. *Everyone had them. Now—how useless.*

"...between the door and the frame. Could use it to get the lock open."

"Think that will work here?"

Christie was aware how cold it was getting. Been chilly all day, but the car had a heater.

But standing here, night falling, it seemed to grow ever more frigid. If they were going to get in, they better do it soon.

Then, "No. This has a dead bolt. No credit card can open that."

"But the back door?"

Christie turned to her daughter.

That could be a different story.

Heavy lock for the front. A kitchen door, though... could maybe just be a simple, door handle lock.

"Worth a try, Kate. Either that, or we'll just have to smash one of the windows."

She looked over to the car where all seemed still, Simon still sleeping. Then a glance out to the dead end street, the nearby houses.

All quiet.

"I'll do it," Kate said.

"No, it's tricky, Kate, I think—"

"Have you ever done it, Mom?"

Christie shook her head.

"And with all that snow you'd have to walk through back there…"

The logic… irrefutable. Christie nodded.

"Think I still have a card or two in my purse." She sniffed at the cold air. "Souvenirs."

Kate smiled.

With every day Kate becoming more her partner in this, less a daughter.

But no, *never less a daughter*. But clearly something more.

Kate hurried back to the car for her mother's wallet.

Then Kate took the card after Christie described the process as best she could.

"And Kate, if the lock is like this one, just come back. Don't keep fiddling back there in the dark."

Kate nodded. "I will…"

And then her daughter turned and dashed toward the back of the house.

Christie waited, standing in the chill, surrounded by dark, wondering how Kate could manage the trick of springing open the back door.

Even if it could be done.

The seconds turning into minutes, and that anxiety, that fear that always seemed right at the surface, started to take over.

She realized that with every day, with the three of them together, she couldn't stand not being able to see her kids.

Every moment.

To protect them.

And maybe—she thought—*protect me.*

Then, a light went on in the back, then another in the hall!

Christie looked at the small, door windows, a trio of them, each no bigger than a paperback novel, as she saw Kate rush to the front, stopping only to throw the switch on a table lamp.

Then, the snap and click of the front door being unlocked.

And she saw Kate grinning.

"I *did* it. It was cool. Just like you said, I worked the card in and out, and finally the door... just slid open."

Kate held the door open so she could walk in and then handed her the now mangled credit card.

"'Course your card is bit messed up."

Christie smiled at her. "No worries about that. Thing's pretty useless these days..." She took the card. "...except for opening doors."

She looked around the living room, seeming as if its owners had gone on vacation, the place left all neat and tidy. The air, chilly—but whatever fuel the boiler still had, the thermostat set low, was keeping the edge off.

Lot of houses around here would have run out of fuel.

And water pipes would explode, those interiors turning into bizarre frozen caves.

But for now, this looked like a home.

She looked at Kate. "Want to go get your brother? Bring him in?"

Christie knew she still needed the cane. But today was better than yesterday, and if she got some rest, took care of the wound again...

Tomorrow will be even better.

"Sure. I'll go get him."

Christie about to say, *Be careful.*

But those words no longer were needed as Kate raced out to the car and her sleeping brother.

22
Jack

Simon had opened the can of peas and then passed the can to Kate, who dumped the peas into a pot. Like the boiler, still enough gas coming from somewhere—propane, maybe lines from the street?—to actually cook them.

Though Christie felt so hungry, she could have eaten them cold right from the can.

Kate stirred them.

"Think I should open a soup as well?" Simon said.

Peas, Christie thought.

Not much of a dinner.

"Really hungry, Simon?"

"A bit…"

She looked away, thinking. Then back to him, "Do you think you can see how you feel after eating this? We want to make all those cans you guys found last."

"Sure."

Kate turned to her. "How do you know they're done?"

"Hmm?"

"The peas. When they're cooked?"

Cooking was never much of a deal back home. So much processed stuff that Christie just heated things up, except for those occasional times when Jack brought home something special.

A scrawny chicken he picked up from a thankful butcher who insisted he take it.

Or some steaks that a family he helped gave him.

Steaks. Seems like a lifetime ago.

"Just have to be warmed up," Christie said. "Probably good now."

Kate nodded, and then her daughter started opening drawers and the cupboard below sink.

"Need one of those thingies…"

"A colander?"

"Yup. Got to be—ah, here it is."

She watched Kate pull out a big metal colander dotted with holes. How many spaghetti dinners had that done service in?

Spaghetti. Meatballs.

Now wouldn't that be something?

Kate poured the peas into the colander over the sink, then took a spoon and ladled the vegetable into three small bowls, each with an ornate flower design running around the edge.

Dinner was served.

*

Christie looked at her kids, scraping their bowls, Simon with a green tinge around his lips, having eaten those peas so fast.

She had suggested opening a second can, just eating half. Something to celebrate their "find."

And also she wanted everyone to linger at the table for a bit.

"Your dad…" she said.

The words halting, catching in her throat. But she had thought about this, the importance of doing *this*.

"He was not a veggie guy."

Her kids both looked up. Christie kept a smile on her face. "In fact, he hated peas. 'Mushy little bowling balls' he called them."

Simon nodded. Kate seemed to be weighing Christie's words, perhaps even wondering *why*.

Why talk of our Dad?

He's gone. We're alone.

Why bring him up?

"When we first met, I was teaching, and of course you could get anything and everything to eat. But he liked his steaks, lobster, and— once in a while—fish, fried flounder."

A nod from Simon.

"How did you meet?"

Christie turned and looked right at her son, thankful for the question.

"Believe it or not, the school I worked in… most schools maybe… had a day where those people who were called—are still called maybe—'first responders' came to the school. Police. Firemen. EMT people—"

"EMT?" Simon said.

Still nothing from Kate, her eyes still seeming to say, *why are we talking about this?*

"Emergency Medical Team. Ambulance people. They all came, talked to the kids, the classes. Had the police cars there, fire trucks, ambulances."

"And Dad saw you?"

Christie nodded, smiling. "Guess so. I was teaching older kids then… Middle school. They didn't care about the special 'guests' in their uniforms, the trucks. They stood around, mostly talking to themselves. But your dad, he stood by his squad car. I saw him. He saw me."

So hard, this, she thought.

"And he walked over and said… something like… 'they don't seem too interested.' I started to apologize for my students. I mean, kids that age. Well, you guys know…"

Did they? Did they have any awareness of just how self-centered kids that age can be, how long they stay that way?

The world revolving around them.

Of course, that world was gone now.

"But he stopped me. And he said, 'Kids, well, they'll be kids.' He asked how long I had been teaching there, did I like the school… you know, just conversation."

Finally Kate spoke up.

"And you liked him?"

She turned and looked right at her daughter.

A small laugh. "Did I? You bet. A handsome cop." Another laugh, and this brought a smile from Kate. "What's… not to like?"

"Then what?" Simon said, completely hooked on the story, this epic of when his parents first met.

A tale probably every kid wants to hear… since—for all of them—that's where it began.

"Oh, a bit more chatting, then I was about to herd my class back into the building when he reached out and—God, I remember it like it was yesterday.

And that is so true.

"He touched my elbow. Just a tap. 'How about dinner some night?' he said. 'Randazzo's in Sheepshead Bay. Ever been?' I hadn't. And your dad said, 'Let's change that.'"

She took a breath.

"We went out for dinner…"

"Have I been there?" Simon asked.

Christie took a breath, the story about to shift, jump years. "When you were a baby. Yes. We went back again. Before all this. You must have been a one-year-old maybe?"

Then, slowly… Kate spoke, "*I remember* that. There were all these boats, and before dinner we walked past them. I remember the smell, all the fish they caught, and people buying them, bunches of them."

"Yup. That's right. The fishing boats in Sheepshead Bay. So many fish." Christie laughed. "And right—it did smell."

Then—and Christie thought she might crumble at this as Kate spoke, "I remember I couldn't see one boat, just docking… everyone gathered around at the end, and you had Simon in a stroller, and,

and… Dad picked me up. Right on his shoulders. So now I was taller than everyone. I could see the whole boat. *All the boats.* It was like I was flying."

Christie saw that Simon had his eyes locked on his sister, picturing that moment that he could not remember.

But nonetheless, he was there.

Kate laughed. "He said to me… Dad said… 'You're as light as one of those fish there.'"

And Christie could picture it as well. The sunny day, changing to dusk, the feeling that for their young family this day was perfect.

She didn't tell her kids that later…

…when they got home, and she gave Simon a bottle, and Jack read to Kate, and all was quiet, that she remembered that they made love.

As if that was the only way to end this perfect day.

The pain of that memory… now so terribly bittersweet.

So, she let the moment and the memories begin to fade.

After all they had been through these past days… weeks…

Months.

…she had felt it was important to summon the spirit of their father, their funny father, their handsome father, their *brave* father who saved them all.

And then gave that responsibility over to her.

Her kids grew quiet. Maybe they sensed that the memory had to fade like smoke, a wonderful fog lifting.

Until she then started talked about plans.

For this very night.

"So, I will keep watch while you guys get some rest," she started. "I can—"

Kate interrupted her.

"Mom, you're the one that needs the rest. I mean, you just left the hospital."

And Christie did feel completely exhausted, the idea of some bed upstairs, waiting… nearly irresistible.

"I'm *fine*. I can always sleep in the car tomorrow. Any problem along the way, you can—"

But Kate shook her head.

"Mom…" her voice strong, a reminder of what her daughter had been through, what she had done already.

A reminder that the three of them were… yes, a family, but also a team.

"I can stand first watch while you sleep."

Simon chimed in. "And I can do it too. I can watch."

She smiled at them. She thought of arguing, telling them that *no, she'd do it*. That she'd be fine.

But one look at Kate's face showed that the argument would not go well.

"Okay. Kate, you can take first watch, then wake me and I—"

"No," Simon said, his voice surprisingly strong. "She can wake me. I can go second. Maybe let you sleep all night…"

Then Christie matched her tone to theirs, even as she was losing this debate. "Listen. All right… I can do a third watch. Okay? We *all* get some rest. We'll need it. But…"

Here she looked at the front door across from such a cozy living room.

"Each of us has to be super-alert. Listen carefully. Anything happens, anything strange at all, wake all of us up. I can set an alarm with my phone—least it's good for something. Three hours each."

Then she looked at the two of them.

"That sound do-able?"

They both nodded.

And though Christie worried about their ability to stay awake and alert, she knew that she herself would struggle with it.

It wasn't the best plan to get through this night.

But it was a plan.

Maybe it would be quiet.

The hamlet of Stormville certainly seemed deserted tonight.

Then, "Peas all done?" she asked.

"Yum," Kate said. "Still some in the can."

Christie laughed. "Okay, Kate, Simon and I will go find some beds. You—well, guess, you'll sit here. Keep your gun close?"

Again, no need for that reminder.

And Christie looked above the fireplace mantel. She saw— inches above the layered stone bricks of the fireplace—an empty rack for a rifle, the weapon now long gone.

She and her kids had weapons, two handguns, and the one rifle they had brought to the hospital.

They had bullets. Christie had so far not counted them.

Because she didn't know what they would do when they were out.

"Okay, Mom. I'll be fine. There's a bookshelf, books. I'll do some reading."

"Get up and stretch if you feel sleepy, Kate, and if you—"

"*Mom*, I'll be fine."

Christie nodded.

"Okay, Simon. Let's go get some sleep."

She grabbed her cane and, using it as leverage to get up, pushed up from the chair with her free hand while holding the metal stick, and then followed Simon as he walked up the blue-carpeted stairs, leaving Kate below.

23
On Kate's Watch

Smiling, Kate had watched her mom and Simon walk upstairs to a stranger's bedrooms.

Though she would have liked to have walked right along with them. She hadn't told her mother, but the driving had left her frazzled, achy even.

And now so tired.

But her mom needed rest; her leg was getting better, but lying down would be good.

And Simon...

She would never say it to him, but she was amazed how for a kid—really, just a kid—he could be so strong.

Was her brother changed forever?

Then, W*ere we all?*

Now it was quiet in this house, this place looking so normal, as if the world hadn't really changed outside.

She went to the living room, and stood by the windows. Her mom had been very clear.

Don't get too near the windows.

Take a peek, but stay well back.

She looked around. Everything neat, orderly. No one had broken into this house after whatever battles had raged in this town.

Standing there, all alone while her mom, her brother, slept, she hoped that there was nothing out there.

That the Can Heads were all gone.

Just the dark, the cold.

And now so alone, she found it hard to hold on to that idea. That belief that this place was deserted.

She took a deep breath, and then walked back over to a large easy chair, a recliner she could tell from a wooden lever by the side.

Sitting down, she felt dwarfed by the chair.

She pushed down on the lever, and the back of the chair tilted back jerkily while a footrest magically appeared.

Then the thought, *Only minutes into her "watch"… could this chair be too comfortable, planting dangerous thoughts of sleep?*

She quickly undid the recline.

A leather-like pouch hung on the side of the chair with three remote controls. She picked one up that looked like it might operate the big screen TV over the fireplace.

She pressed a green button.

A flickering noise, but the giant screen remained dark. She pressed the "up" arrow, then down to move through channels as the TV screen remained blank.

Not that she expected anything else.

She guessed it had been such a long time since the last broadcast of *Adult Swim* or *The Vampire Diaries.* And those shows… always repeats, even back home on Staten Island.

No new shows. Not after the Can Heads.

And so many nights, the TV dead. No cable. No Wi-Fi.

As if such things never existed.

She guessed there might be DVDs around here somewhere— some people probably still watched them—maybe a player near the TV.

Instead, she got out of the over-padded chair and walked into the kitchen.

She opened the refrigerator without putting the kitchen light on.

The insides had been picked clean, and since their arrival this evening, they had only put a half-empty can of peas inside.

No refrigeration needed for all the other random canned goods that were supposed to keep them fed.

For how long ?

That was always the question.

She shut the door.

While back at the Mountain Inn—as terrible as it was there, with all those men looking at her and no doubt what they were thinking—at least it had been a place to stay.

To sleep.

But then that place had been overrun, Simon nearly captured by people—regular... people, if that's what they really were—who decided that living like a Can Head was not such a bad idea.

People had to eat.

The memories... made her shiver.

But walking out of the kitchen, she realized that when she thought about their future, *her* future, what was there?

The hope of meeting up with people trying to build a life, so far away... Michigan!

Really? Might as well be Mars.

Could they really get there? And even if they did, what would they find?

She shook her head as if that could make these worries fly away. Then again out to the living room, only lit by the yellow light of a table lamp beside the recliner.

She saw all the books on the bookshelf.

Never been much of reader.

She liked her music. She liked watching her shows when they were on.

Reading... seemed difficult.

Now—not much choice.

She walked over to the built-in wooden shelves.

She didn't recognize any of the books. The titles—meaningless. All seemed old, many with their dust covers frayed, while those without covers had the stern, dark binding of the hymnals from the small Episcopalian church they used to go to on the big holidays.

Christmas. Easter.

Just the big holidays.

God—not much of a thing for them.

Seemed so long ago.

She ran her fingers over the spines, looking for a title, something that would make her want to slide one of the books out.

Then she came across one that—for some reason—she seemed to remember hearing about.

Had her mother read it? Or her dad?

Though she didn't remember seeing him with a book either. Her dad liked to tinker with the car, do things in the garage, and, and...

She stopped that train of thought.

She slid the book out.

Gone With the Wind.

She nodded.

Yes, that title certainly seemed right, though she didn't have a clue what the book was about.

Gone with the Wind.

Like everything. All gone, after a terrible wind blew through the world.

She brought the book with its dark, maroon binding back to the chair.

Probably going to be completely boring, she thought.

She opened the book, flicked through the blank pages, the title page, to Chapter One.

And read:

Scarlett O'Hara was not beautiful, but men seldom realized it when caught by her charm as the Tarleton twins were.

Hmm, she thought. Interesting way to begin a story...

*

Hours later, Kate looked up at the big clock on the fireplace mantel.

She had become so caught up in Scarlett, her world—and all her suitors!—that she forgot she was supposed to wake up Simon for his watch.

And since this novel of Tara, and the war, and those amazing dresses and men in uniforms had taken her completely away from this town, this house, her life...

This ugly, deadly world.

She made a vow: She'd always have a book with her.

Because that's what books can do.

But with an awareness of the time, she now felt her own fatigue come roaring back.

She needed to awaken Simon, make sure he was okay.

Things had been so quiet. She barely was aware of her gun sitting on the coffee table.

She found a coaster and slid it into the book as a bookmark, closed it, and then started up the stairs.

24
Simon Alone

Simon had been dreaming.

He had been back at that castle-like hotel, hiding under the bed, when those men came.

In real life, he hid; they didn't find him.

Now, with it feeling so real, in his dream he watched as their feet moved around the room, their faces unseen, lingering, opening doors talking, grunting.

He wanted the dream to end.

Even as it was going on, he knew it wasn't happening. But that didn't help. Maybe this… nightmare *was* real.

Maybe he never escaped.

Then, one of the men fell to the floor on his knees to look under the bed, and Simon saw his eyes, bulging, crisscrossed with red lines, the mouth gaping open as he barked out words.

"He's here! The boy's *here!*"

The man reached out to touch Simon, to grab him, and—

Simon felt that hand closing on his shoulder, then a voice.

"Simon…"

Kate, his sister.

Her voice low, the room dark—the man, the room, the nightmare fading.

"It's time, Simon. Your turn."

For a minute he didn't have an idea what she was talking about. What did she mean by "turn?" To do… what?

Then, with Kate's hand still on his shoulder, he remembered everything, all of it coming in bits and pieces. The town they were in, this house they found, the food, the bear, and—

It was his turn.

To get up and stand watch.

There would have been a time when he would have said that he was too tired, that he didn't want to get up.

But he knew that he couldn't say those words anymore. They were together, a team. Kate, sitting on the bed now, had saved him.

And his mother needed him.

He rubbed his eyes, partly thankful that his sister's waking him up had at least ended that nightmare.

"Want me to turn on a light?" Kate asked.

He nodded, then realizing it was too dark for her to see… "Sure."

His mom was asleep in another bedroom so they wouldn't wake her.

Though he'd have to wake her up in a few hours.

He sat up in bed.

"Everything… go okay?" he asked.

"So quiet," she said. "It's a ghost town," Kate said, smiling.

But Simon wished that she hadn't used those words.

Ghost town.

He started to sluggishly get out of the warm bed. The house felt cold, the floor on his bare feet icy.

"You going to be okay?" Kate asked again.

Simon stood up, picking up his socks from the floor, a sweater he had peeled off. He had slept in his jeans, but even with them on his legs felt cold in this chill.

"Can I put on some heat?"

"I have it on low. Not sure how much fuel this place has left. So maybe… just leave it. Can you do that?"

A nod.

Then down to grab his sneakers.

He kept having to push away the idea that the only thing he wanted in all the world was to go back to bed.

"You wake mom in two and a half hours. It will go fast," Kate said.

Simon wasn't sure about that at all.

He started for the door out of the bedroom while Kate began to slip into the still-warm bed.

And as he walked out she said quietly, "You're a good kid, Simon."

He nodded.

He shut the door behind him as he entered the hallway and the stairs leading down.

First thing he did was to check his gun. Funny how important that had become to him.

A gun, bullets.

Just part of his daily life.

It had been sitting on the coffee table, next to Kate's handgun.

A year ago he would have found this to be something out of a movie, even though—like everyone—he knew what was going on outside their fenced-in community.

Now... this was totally normal.

But he didn't put the gun back; instead, he carried it as he walked around the house now, barrel down like his dad had taught him.

Like my dad taught me, he thought.

The safety on.

He was all set. He thought he should check all the windows in the house first.

But the rumbling in his stomach sent him out to the kitchen, to the refrigerator.

He opened the door and said to himself, "More peas! Oh boy..."

He finished the can. There had only been a few tablespoons in the can, and—now cold—they tasted weird. Not like peas at all, but some slushy mushy stuff.

But simply eating made him feel better.

There was also soup, and some other vegetables in the canned goods they'd found.

I could easily eat more, he thought.

But then, *We have to make the food last.*

And when they got to where they were going, to Michigan—wherever that was—his mom had said there'd be other things, better things.

Real food, he thought.

Then he wandered out to the living room.

Everything so quiet.

His mom, sister, dead asleep upstairs. Outside, nothing. The only noise was the hum of the refrigerator.

He guessed he could put a DVD in—he saw them on a shelf, but then he thought, *If I'm watching a movie, I won't hear things.*

And wasn't that why he was awake, standing guard?

Listening, alert.

Still, he had to do something for the next few hours.

He thought about his old action figures, gathered together in a plastic bag, all from different movies. A few dinosaurs. Luke Skywalker and two robots. An alien with its giant head and teeth.

An Indiana Jones that his father had said had once been his.

That was his favorite—just a guy with a rubbery bullwhip, stopping the others… stopping *dinosaurs*!

He guessed he could play with them. Hadn't felt like even looking at them now for a while.

Gotten too old for them, he thought.

Too old for toys.

But now, tonight… it seemed like good idea.

And he walked over to the hallway where he had dropped his backpack, and he dug out the figures.

*

The furniture made for good mountains and cliffs.

The dinosaurs would chase Indy, and he could lean over the side of a seat cushion and then use his whip to catch invisible branches and ledges to swing down to safety.

And when Indy swung to the top of the sofa-mountain—to the highest point at the back of the chair, cornered by the hungry alien—the Indy figure could spin around with a crack of the whip, just like Simon saw in the movie, and send the monster flying down to the rocky sea below.

And it would land on the plush carpet and bounce.

The fact that no one was around to watch him playing, to watch him being a kid again, made this easier.

It was—despite how late at night it was—fun.

And the living room had so many places to climb, to explore, for the action figures to hide.

Lot of adventures to be had here!

But eventually, Simon stopped.

Like something creeping up on him, then suddenly it was *there...*

He felt so tired.

Maybe he could find a DVD for the otherwise useless TV? But instead, he looked at the clock on the wall.

Only a little more than an hour left before he'd wake his mom.

Maybe he could just sit in the chair for a while.

Sitting would feel good. The sofa, once a mountain, now looking so comfortable.

He gathered his figures together and dumped them at one end. Maybe they'd start a battle or two while he just sat there, rather than him scrambling around the whole room on his knees.

He plopped down on the couch, pounding one of the pillows so that he could lay back.

The thought occurred to him that it was *too* comfortable.

Then, *I really should get up. Not a good idea to lie down like this.*

And that was his last thought...
Before he heard a noise that woke him up.

25
Visitors

The noise hadn't been loud, just loud enough in the terrible quiet that it made Simon blink awake, heart thumping.

For a moment, he didn't know where he was. The living room—where was this place?

But his life, for all these months, had been all about strange new places.

Then his eyes went to the coffee table, and the handgun sitting on it.

Gun right there, just feet away.

But that noise...

He sat up, slowly, as though he himself might make a big sound just in sitting up.

He swung his legs off the cushions—he realized that he had been fully lying down, and had fallen deeply asleep.

A look to the clock. His mom had another twenty minutes. Still, if that sound was *something*, maybe he should wake her, go get her up early.

But what if it was nothing?

Then again. Cracking sounds, like gravel being walked on.

Now he felt his heart begin to race even more. And he leaned forward and, taking care to do so quietly, he slid the gun off the table, barrel pointed down.

A check that the safety was on.

He was tempted to click the safety off.

But that was not the rule. Safety on, until it absolutely had to be thrown off.

The rules were important; the rules let them live.

Instead, he stood up, his ears cocked. Maybe the sound would go away.

Could be an animal, he thought. After all, they had seen a bear today. They had actually killed a bear today!

So wild animals had managed to stay alive around here.

Bet that's what it is, he thought.

But when the sound didn't come back, he felt his breathing become normal as he stood like a statue in the room.

Quickly, he thought, *It was nothing.*

And to prove it—and to show himself that he was doing a good job at this, even though he had fallen asleep—he walked over to the front windows.

Pausing a few steps away from the glass that, with no lights outside, looked black.

Then he leaned close, trying to see into the inky blackness.

But there was nothing, even as he looked left, then right.

He saw the outline of their car. Then trees. Farther away, the other houses, all dark.

Whatever had made the sound, it was gone.

Sure.

But then, the noise again, a bumping sound.

This time, from the back of the house, near the kitchen.

Still no reason to wake anybody, he thought.

But he best walk back there and check that door, look out those windows.

Simon turned away from the living room windows and started walking back.

He walked to the door so slowly, his gun pointed down, safety on.

Just like Dad taught me.

To the back door. Small curtains on either side of the window, blackness in the back.

To what? A backyard? Was there a swing set? Or maybe a sandbox? Or maybe the people here had no kids. Maybe just a lawn, now frozen hard. A barbecue that would have become useless.

Lots of useless things in this world.

He expected to hear the sound again, so he stopped, just feet from the window.

He licked his lips.

He had been scared plenty of times. Back at the inn. The night they escaped the hospital.

The bear.

But that was all in the past. This was now, and he could feel something that in some ways was worse than any of that.

The... *not knowing.*

Was there anything there? Something else to be scared of? Or was it just a sound in the night?

With his free hand he rubbed his eyes.

I'm so tired too, he told himself.

That might have something to do with it.

He waited, and was going to walk back to the living room, hoping that time would race to the moment when he could finally wake up his mom and crawl back in bed.

But—the thought—he *really* should look.

Better check.

And so he bent close to the door's windows, not seeing much better now with his face close to the glass.

No, just more inky blackness out there.

He saw nothing else.

There's nothing there, he told himself.

And he turned away from the door, ready to walk quickly back to the living room.

To his action figures suspended on cliffs, ready to swim rivers made by a rug, all the lights on, nice and bright.

He turned his back on the door.

He didn't even take a step before he heard the crash—a great shattering of glass and wood as something burst through the door's windows behind him.

At the same moment, he began raising his gun.

Safety's on, he thought. *Have to get the safety off.*

But all that was too slow, his arm much too slow for what had broken through the windows and then—so fast—he felt a hand...

Had to be a hand.

...close, tight on his neck, and *squeezing.*

Air stopped immediately—he had been in mid-gasp, ready to yell even as he tried to raise the gun.

Now he couldn't breathe. And he made a mistake.

He brought his hand up to try to unwrap those fingers that seemed so strong, so tight on his neck, his own hand feeling so small.

Clawed at that grasping hand.

But then his arm was grabbed, yanking him back to the door. He felt some jagged glass cut into the back of his head.

The more he struggled, the tighter he felt held.

And with his right arm pinned, there was no way he could get the safety off, though he tried to flip it with his thumb even as he writhed—a prisoner.

Seconds. That's all the time it took. The kitchen seemed to glow as if on fire. Everything wavering, blurry as he clawed against those hands that held him.

He knew what they belonged to.

A Can Head.

And once he stopped struggling...

Once he was dead.

The Can Head would find a way in. Would eat him.

Or maybe it would somehow sense that there were other people here, and while they slept, creep up to his mother, Kate...

Simon could turn his head back a bit, and just make out a dirt-encrusted face. Whatever it had eaten in the past, a victim's blood, thick and dark, covering that face like paint.

The glow of the kitchen—now a fire.

And as much as he had felt the need to struggle, now he felt like he should stop.

Had to stop.

Had to just let it end.

With his eyes on the thing's head, seeing those mad eyes wide with hunger.

Cartoon eyes. Bulging.

So eager.

Then, he saw something else.

Two hands. Massive hands, dark hands catching the kitchen light. And those hands landed on either side of the Can Head's head.

The bulging eyes now aware of something.

Simon heard his gun fall to the floor.

Suddenly too heavy to hold up.

And then—so fast—those black hands gave the head a sharp twist.

Like the cap coming off a ketchup bottle.

Left, and then fast, to the right again.

And immediately—like something unlocking—the hand wrapped tight around Simon's neck sprang free.

His right arm was also released as the Can Head's other claw hand let that slip away as well.

Until Simon could stagger away from the door, gulping the air, coughing, even spitting on the floor.

Bent over.

And when that coughing had ended, when he finally stood up straight again, he saw a different face at the door's smashed window.

The face, now lit by kitchen light: dark, round, like a black moon. The eyes small, squinting as if they had just been in the dark for a long time.

And the man at the window spoke.

"You... okay?"

And Simon nodded, and for a moment did nothing but look at the man, the big round face, the small smile that appeared after Simon nodded.

26
Ben

Christie woke up.

She had that moment, wondering—*Where am I, where am I sleeping?*—before she remembered.

Then the pieces of the day came flying back, like sticky notes that had blown away and needed to be recovered.

Remembering... finding the food. Finding this house. The plan to take shifts, sleeping, watching.

And in the dark room—under these covers that belonged to some unknown people, pulled tight, keeping her warm in the chilly house—she heard voices.

First Simon's voice.

Then a deep voice. A laugh. The words indistinct.

But then, now fully awake, remembering how she got to this bed, she was also aware that someone was down there with Simon.

She reached down beside her bed and felt the wooden stock of her gun.

The thought incomprehensible, *My son down there, talking to someone.*

She took care getting out of bed. Old houses, and the floorboards, would creak. And the room was dark. She'd have to navigate an unfamiliar space. That is, unless she put the light on.

Won't do that, she thought.

No.

Standing up, her feet cold despite the socks, picking up the gun carefully, feeling so heavy when she had simply been lying in bed, just holding the covers tight.

The sounds again. Simon's voice, then the other voice, so deep.

She started to the door, open enough that its outline caught some of the light from below.

A step.

She flipped the rifle's safety off. The *click* sounding so loud in the small bedroom.

And she kept walking to the stairs leading down.

The voices came from the kitchen, and now Christie could catch a few words.

Simon: "But what did you do then?"

Then a deep laugh—so deep—and: "I didn't know what to do, now with everyone gone."

Christie could feel her heart racing. On one hand she felt glad that it sounded like Simon was all right.

On the other, who the hell was he talking to? Why would he let someone into this house?

Without asking me.

She walked past the living room and then, slowly, into the kitchen, not raising her rifle but keeping it at a forty-five-degree angle.

Ready.

And she saw Simon and someone else sitting at the small kitchen table.

The stranger saw her first.

A giant of a man, six-feet-plus tall, but also wide. His head bald, an oval face.

He had been smiling, talking—but his dark face froze when he saw her.

And Simon spun around fast.

"Mom?" he said.

"Simon," she said quietly, keeping her voice as steady as she could. "Simon, what's going on?"

Then she looked at the back door. Dish towels jammed into the door's broken windows, and on the floor, a pile of shattered glass, swept to a corner of the kitchen.

"Mom," Simon said. "This is Ben."

Christie nodded.

Right, Ben.

As if that made perfect sense that Simon would be sitting here, chatting with someone.

She saw that Simon's gun sat on the table, right there, certainly close enough that this Ben could reach over and grab it.

Then the man—his face still frozen, apparently sensing Christie's alarm—started to stand up.

"I'm sorry, ma'am," he said slowly. "I didn't mean—"

But Simon interrupted him.

Simon's voice now strong. "Mom, he saved my life."

Christie's eyes went from her son, to Ben, and back again.

The man remained standing there.

"Maybe I should go. Maybe leave..." he went on.

He started to turn, and now Simon stood up. "Mom! He *saved* my life."

And Christie had the thought, *When does all this become too much for me?*

And not for the first time, she hated—in some strange way— how her husband left all this for her to deal with.

She would have given anything for Jack to be here. Now.

To be in charge.

Instead, she took more steps toward the table.

It was Simon who noticed first. Christie had been so scared.

"Mom, you're not using your cane."

Had she been that scared?

Christie nodded, moving to a chair, a plain wooden-back chair that matched the simple wooden kitchen table pressed tight against the wall.

"Sit down," she said. To Simon, to Ben.

And she took that chair, taking a breath.

A little after 3 a.m. She had gotten a good five hours sleep.

And that would be all for this night, as she asked, "What happened?"

Simon had arched his neck up, showing a visible purple mark.

The place where the Can Head had grabbed him.

Ben sat silently as Simon breathlessly finished the tale: how Ben appeared, and just twisted the Can Head's head one way, then the other, and it was all over.

"So... I asked him in. I gave him—"

Simon pointed to a can on the counter by the sink. French string beans.

"He was hungry."

Ben nodded in confirmation of that fact, and Christie had the realization that Ben... had some issues.

So big, massively strong, and yet so quiet here, like a school child.

Finally she looked up to him.

"Ben, thank you for saving Simon."

The words sounding absurd.

But not absurd at all in this world.

She reached out and covered Simon's hand. She knew that with all that her kids had to deal with, she had to be as strong a possible. There was no room for weakness.

Ben nodded. "That's okay, Mrs.—"

"Christie," she said, with a smile.

He smiled at that. "I usually don't see too many of them around. Those Can Heads. When all the people left, those things... it seemed they left too."

Christie looked over at Simon who, with a glance, told her that he understood that Ben—what was the word?

Struggled?

"Brave of you to come, and help…"

He shook his head. "Normally, I'd have gone in the other direction. Fast as I could. Fighting even *one* of them can be hard. But… but I saw that it had something… someone it was holding. Couldn't walk away then."

His head bobbed up and down, as if that was a universal truth.

But Christie guessed many a normal person would have done just that, move as fast away as possible in the other direction.

"So, Ben, what happened here, in this town? Why are you still here?"

Ben's face scrunched up, the question making him think and remember.

"You mean to all the people? They went to other places."

Christie nodded, then quickly to Simon, "Simon, you want to grab some more sleep?"

But her son shook his head.

"I want to hear too."

Of course, she thought.

So much to know, to understand—and Simon needed to have it all.

"Okay," Ben said quietly his long pause resolved, his answer ready.

"I used to work… in the Stop & Shop, the big food store on the highway? A big place," he went on, explaining.

"I know," Christie smiled. "A really big store."

"I got all the carts. The ones people just leave after they load their cars, and I push them back to the store."

Another pause. She and Simon said nothing.

"I liked my job. The people… they were nice to me. The customers, well some just in a hurry. But a lot would smile. Say, 'How you doin', Ben?"

Then, repeating it, "I liked it."

More silence.

"Then everything changed."

27
The Road Ahead

Christie thought it was amazing to see the world of the Can Heads through the eyes of this man who corralled shopping carts for a living.

His storytelling slow, the man still wrestling with how the world changed.

"Then the store... it would only open certain hours. And they had guards, with guns, and a big fence. Fences everywhere! But in the small house I stayed in, it seemed quiet."

Christie could imagine this hamlet nestled away, with locals on guard, protected for a while from the mayhem that surrounded the cities.

"But then people started disappearing—they just disappeared—and then other people came! They started fighting each other, regular people, but fighting each other. I didn't understand that. They weren't Can Heads... didn't look like Can Heads."

He paused. Then, "And they took people..."

He shook his head then, catching his mistake. "No, not people. The kids. They took kids, Mrs.... Christie."

She nodded.

And what Christie hoped had been an isolated phenomenon, what they had seen at that camp, in the mountains, was not.

We don't just have Can Heads to worry about now.

Christie stood up, and turned to Simon.

"You can get a few hours' sleep before we get going—I'm on watch now."

At the same time Ben stood up, nodding.

"And I... I better go. Things can get strange out here... when night ends, and day comes."

But she saw Simon didn't move.

He only said, "Mom."

And she knew what he was thinking.

We can't just let this guy go out there as if nothing happened.

Not after what he did.

But then, how much food did they have? Could they really—what?—bring him with them?

Ben was already moving to the front door.

And again Simon hadn't moved and only repeated, *"Mom."*

And she nodded.

There were times, even these days, when one simply had to do the right thing.

"Ben—"

The man stopped. He held his old parka, torn in spots, in his right hand. In his left, a deep maroon beanie.

Amazing that he had been able to live on his own.

"Ben, how about you come with us?"

At first, the only expression on the man's face was surprise... or maybe confusion.

"What? I don't—"

Christie walked to him, Simon at her heels.

"We're going someplace... Michigan. It's another state. Still days from here. Supposedly people living there. Going to try to grow food, to protect themselves."

Ben nodded. Christie was not at all sure he understood what she was saying.

"You should come with us. There's nothing for you here."

148

Ben was silent. She didn't know if the offer was simply overwhelming… or if Ben was just trying to understand what it meant.

A safe place. Food to be grown.

Michigan.

Did that mean anything to him?

Then Christie saw him gulp.

"What do you say, Ben?"

Simon went to him.

"You gotta come with us."

The man looked down at her son.

And she spotted a glistening in his eyes.

All the months he had spent out here, alone, surviving somehow. Now being invited to join her family.

Even though Christie couldn't be sure how all this would turn out.

Talk about one day at a time.

Again, "What do you say, Ben?"

And he nodded. Then, simply, "I'd like that."

Then his face brightened, the decision made, offer accepted. "And I have some food I found. I can bring that! Even pretzels!" he said, his grin widening.

"Great," Christie said. "Why don't you lie down for a bit, then? We'll leave in the morning. Get some rest."

She hefted the gun. "I'll be watching out for everyone."

And despite the fact the man had saved her son, Christie realized that they knew nothing about him, save what he said about his life here.

And now… he was with them.

Still, despite a flicker of concern, it seemed like the right decision.

"Okay," Ben said, following her command.

Simon looked up and smiled.

"I'll go get some sleep too," Simon said heading to the stairs.

And in a few moments, Christie was alone, kitchen lights on, with a quiet house—save for what was maybe the loudest snore she ever heard rumbling from the living room.

*

Christie had waited an additional hour after dawn. Bit more sleep for Kate, for them all.

The hours she was awake had seemed interminable, watching the dark sky lighten, going so slowly as if sunrise might never arrive.

Until a brilliant sun cut through trees to the east, the sun still low in the sky but the light wonderful.

Then it was time to get going.

And Kate, shuffling downstairs, ready for a day of driving, didn't hide her concern over the new member of their party.

"Mom, *what* are you thinking? We don't have much food. And who knows what's ahead, and you ask a guy... that *big* to join us?"

Christie shook her head.

"A bit more quietly, please. He does have ears, you know."

But Ben was talking to Simon in the living room and Christie guessed that he really couldn't hear them.

"And what do you know about him?"

Christie shook her head. "Not much. But he was there last night, when your brother needed him."

That seemed to stop Kate.

Being there... such an important idea.

Kate had been there for all of them. They wouldn't be here, alive, if not for her.

And Christie had said that they make all decisions together.

Kate shook her head.

"I bet he eats a lot."

Christie smiled. "Looks that way. But says he has some food he's been hiding, things he found after everyone left."

Then to nudge Kate toward some acceptance, "Simon wanted it. I think... that's important."

Another nod from Kate. Not on board, but finally accepting the new passenger.

"He seems quite sweet," Christie said. "Innocent, despite all the things he must have seen."

"Sure," Kate said.

Christie half-expected a *whatever*.

Instead...

"We all set to go?"

"I heated some soup. Have some."

"I'm okay now," Kate said. "Guess... bring what's leftover with us. We're going to need everything."

Christie nodded. She didn't like it when even a tiny bit of a wall went up between her and her daughter.

She so needed Kate to get through this.

Then Kate—the driver, really the person in charge now—walked out to the living room.

"Simon..." then, hesitant, "Ben... you guys all set to go?"

Christie stayed in the kitchen, watching, as Ben turned.

"Y-yes," he said. "Maybe we can pick up my food on the way?"

"Sure," Kate said. "We can always use more food."

And if there was an edge to Kate's comment, she was sure Ben didn't pick up on it.

Then Kate turned to her. "Time to get going."

And they all started moving to the front door, to what looked like a glorious morning, leaving this warm house that was just another place they passed, on their way to whatever was ahead.

28
Roadblock

Christy looked down at the map.

The road ahead, Route 6.

That should have taken them well into western Pennsylvania. Now it looked like it had been slammed by a tornado. Trees down, burnt-out cars on either side.

Kate gamely plowed her way through the debris, curving through the literal log jam.

But at this rate, it would be a week, maybe even more, before they reached the eastern end of Michigan.

And she knew they couldn't afford that.

"Mom, this is no good," Kate said, stating the obvious.

It didn't help that Kate could still drive jerkily, giving the car a little gas, then braking, turning... her moves not at all smooth.

Christie looked at her daughter, hands grimly locked on the wheel. Christie felt that soon she could take over some of the driving.

But not on this road, not driving like this.

On the map, she saw the interstate highway, I-80, so close.

No choice now.

They'd just have to backtrack, get on the big highway, get away from all this.

They'd have to ignore all the dangers of being on a highway.

She looked back at Simon,... Ben.

Simon asleep, head against a window. Ben, a giant in the back seat, a gentle smile on his face.

Then back, "Kate, I think we should get on the interstate."

Anther jerky brake as Kate turned, looked, then back to the latest barrier that had to be passed.

"But, Mom, you said the highways… they're dangerous. I mean, remember…"

Christie could.

The gas station.

When they were on their way to the Paterville camp, to their lives being changed forever.

They survived the fact that the place had been taken over by Can Heads.

But then this thought, *Back then we had Jack.*

He had been there.

Now it was just them.

"Don't think we have a choice, Kate. We can't waste so much time, doing this, using up the food. And these towns… I mean, they look all empty. But what if we hit one, winding our way through… that wasn't?"

But Kate had already nodded, accepting the logic.

My partner in all this, Christie thought.

"Okay. What do I do? How do we get there?"

"Okay. You have to turn around and—"

"Really? Go *back?* After—"

Christie reached over and touched her daughter's hand, the knuckles white from her firm grip on the steering wheel.

What a way to learn to drive.

"It's not far. There's a road that takes you to an on-ramp. Won't be long."

Another nod from Kate.

Then she laughed. "Um, not sure I know how to turn around."

Christie laughed as well.

"Right. Okay. It's called a three—point turn. So first, back up..." Christie turned around to see how much leeway the car had going in reverse. "...slowly, about a car length or two, and then I'll coach you from there."

And Christie kept looking back as Kate backed the car up, too fast, then followed by an equally jarring slamming of the brakes.

"Now, cut the wheel right. And Kate—just the tip of your toes, a little bit of gas..."

And somehow, Kate managed it... and they were on their way, back where they came from, back to find the highway.

When they got to the highway, Christie saw the on-ramp, a single lane leading to a toll booth with its barrier missing.

Probably someone smashed right through it.

Toll booths. They belong to a different world.

And as soon as they were on the empty highway, already that felt chilling, eerie—no other cars, only the occasional spotting of a deserted, abandoned car or the black curlicues of tires that had spun off eighteen-wheelers.

She had told Kate, *"I think I can drive soon. Leg's feeling pretty good."*

Kate nodded, turned to her. *"You sure?"*

She had patted her daughter's hand. Kate had done so well with this, but it was time to give her a break.

And truth was, she was feeling better, especially with the ability to use cruise control on the empty highway. Not much stress on the leg at all.

After a few hours on the road, they stopped.

She got one of the plastic gas containers from the trunk—five gallons—and poured it all into the tank.

Did they have enough to get all the way to Michigan?

Not even close.

But she'd deal with what when they had to.

And then—with a touch to Kate's cheek—a smile.

"Thanks, Kate. Time for you to rest."

And Christie began driving.

*

The drive... monotonous. Simon awake, looking out the window; Ben and Kate both sleeping.

In a few hours she'd have to think what they'd do for the night.

The night—that was always a question.

Where would it be safe?

That idea itself seemed absurd.

The cruise control kept the car moving at a steady sixty miles per hour. She barely had to steer except to avoid the random junk—a hubcap, an exploded piece of luggage, its contents spread all over the road.

All suggesting grim stories.

She knew the risk they were taking in travelling on the exposed highway, bottled up between exits.

Every now and then she turned on the radio, volume low, and scanned for a station.

Once she picked up a snippet of something, but with so much static that only a smattering of words was intelligible.

She did register one near-complete sentence.

"...*have been no further... from the state government. People are advised*—"

Then gone.

People are advised.

Then the highway passed by a row of industrial buildings, a huge complex, no indication of what their purpose was, just massive gray stone structures close to the road.

Doubtful anything worthwhile could be in them.

She couldn't afford chasing wild geese.

Though, she admitted to herself, this whole escape to a place that might only be a rumor could be just that.

She had to keep reminding herself to stay in this moment, deal with what's going on.

Anything else, and she might lose it.

She took a breath. Something she remembered back from her days before the kids, taking yoga classes. Breathing. Trying to stay calm, keep focused.

When—ahead—down a long, straight strip of the highway, she now saw something stretching clear across the highway.

She gently tapped the brake.

Killing cruise control.

Her eyes locked on what was ahead, now closer.

Close enough to see...

A wall of cars stretching across the highway, a blockade.

She let the car slow, glanced in the rearview mirror at Simon in the back.

No one awake now.

And she knew that all the steady breathing in the world wouldn't keep her calm.

29
Boxed In

Kate leaned forward.

"Mom, what is it?"

Christie said nothing. She just put the car into reverse and started backing up. She'd have to edge the vehicle to the side of the road, then turn around.

She looked in the rearview mirror to check on Simon. He too was awake, eyes wide.

Like my kids can now sense danger, as if they're changing into some other kind of human.

And that, though, was more than a little scary.

But then, just above Simon, in the back windshield, she saw a black SUV, a big one, one of those giant Fords, or maybe an Escalade, racing toward her.

And she realized what this was.

They had a wall to stop her one way.

And that car coming toward her to keep her from getting away.

She backed up faster since there was nothing else to do, except to try and get away.

And as soon as she felt her car hit the dirt and dried grass off the pavement, she quickly went into forward, but unable to resist a glance in the mirror again, the black car so much closer.

Kate had noticed too, turning in her seat.

Which triggered Simon, now unbuckled, kneeling, looking out the back window.

"Simon," she said, "Sit down. I can't see. And buckle up, damn it."

She gunned the car forward, and she felt that move in her wounded leg.

She was okay for steady highway driving. But this jerking backward and forward, racing to the right, then left, the wheels screeching like they were out of a stupid cop chase movie... it was too much.

And when she finally made that hard turn, thinking that the car would almost roll over, the curve so tight and the accelerator floored.

Christie saw the SUV had changed direction and now was aimed at her like a missile.

She cut right, avoiding some black rubber treads in the center lane, and saw the SUV adjust as well.

Locked on. Racing to her.

"Mom!" Kate said. "They're coming right at us."

And feeling so helpless; she cut to the left, the SUV doing the same thing.

In another few feet, she'd be unable to avoid a headlong crash.

The SUV could probably weather that.

Her car would be crumpled like a paper napkin, her kids wedged in a trap of metal and glass.

She took her foot off the accelerator.

Simon: "Mom, what are you doing?"

Christie kept her eyes locked on the SUV, and as her car slowed, she noticed the SUV—still aimed right at her—also hit the brakes, a puff of smoke erupting from its rear tires.

Until it too slowed, and the two vehicles slowly rolled within a hundred feet of each other, nose to nose.

And then—fully stopped. Christie's mind raced, trying to think what she should do.

This car in front of her.

All those others in back.

Had she come this far with her kids to have it all end like this?

Then the final, crushing thought: *What would her husband do?*
God, what would Jack do?

She said the only idea she had.

"Kids…"

The words always absurd.

Her eyes tearing.

"Have your guns ready. Safeties off."

Christie's rifle was to her left, stuck like a road map between the seat cushion and the door.

Releasing the steering wheel, her left hand went down, and—with a click—released the safety, and she kept her hand there while she waited.

The black SUV just sat there, nothing happening for a moment.

"Is everything okay?" Ben asked, his innocent question almost welcome when clearly everything was not okay.

"Not sure, Ben. Just going to wait a minute, see what happens."

Kate looked at her, her face set.

But whether her daughter was worried about scaring Simon or didn't want to unnerve Christie any more than she was, she said nothing.

Then, the driver and passenger doors of the black SUV opened.

Two men got out, rifles in their hands, barrels raised. They stood there a moment, perhaps to see what response that move would bring.

"What should we do?" Kate said, so quietly.

"Just… wait," Christie said, not having much belief in that plan.

Thinking, *Maybe with the men out of the vehicle, I should try to get past them.*

It would take them a while to hop back in, turn around and, and…

And *what?*

In minutes, they could be behind her, now maybe with guns

out.

If she did that move, it would be when there was nothing else to do.

She realized that she was slowly taking in one breath then letting go, as if somehow that could miraculously keep her calm.

Then men started walking toward her car, separated by five... six feet, walking slowly.

Guns not pointed, but at a "ready" angle, just like Jack had taught her.

Ready to rear up a few inches and blast away.

And now closer, she saw that one of the guns wasn't an ordinary rifle. One was some kind of machine gun, an automatic weapon.

Pull the trigger, and it could spray them with bullets.

"You know those people?" Ben said, and even his voice sounded nervous now.

"No, Ben. I don't."

More steps and then—with the men only yards away—they stopped.

The men could easily look in her car. She saw them turn to each other, say something, then back to the car.

One man made a gesture, rolling his right hand, a sign to open a window.

Christie hit the button and her window came down. Then she quickly hit the button to stop it at just the halfway point.

"Lady, what... what the *hell* you doing out here?"

Then the other man, "You've been following us?"

She shook her head.

She lowered the window some more.

"No. We didn't know you were there. We just want to move on now. So if you could—"

One man shook his head.

Then words that made Christie's stomach go tight.

"You best get out of the car."

She gulped.

"Mom…" Kate said.

"We just want to go back. We'll stay…" She hunted for words that would appease them. "…away from you, from this highway. Just let us…"

Then, so slowly, one of the men started to raise his rifle.

"Best you get out of the car. So we can talk. All of you."

Christie shook her head.

The idea of starting the car, and racing away, now seemed like the only option.

But then… to race past them? Bullets firing at them?

The very definition of hopeless.

Then the other man, his automatic weapon now also raised, barked, "Get out now. All of you!"

Christie turned to Kate, Simon… and even Ben's moon-like face now crossed with lines of worry.

She cleared her throat.

"We have to get out. We got to do it, kids."

She expected an argument.

But to neutralize that, she quickly popped open her own door and released her hand from her gun, swung her legs over the metal barrel and suddenly stood outside.

She looked back at the kids, doing nothing. Frozen.

She turned back to the men.

"They're just kids. Why can't you just let us go?"

The men stood there.

Until one of them said, "Kids? Then you should damn well be scared, lady."

What is he talking about?

She heard a door pop open. Kate getting out, standing right by the open door. But Christie saw that she still held her gun in her hand.

Then another pop, and Simon, then Ben, got out.

The wind whipped around them. The temperature in the forties, but the chill still so strong.

Christie looked back at the men.

"Can we go? We just want—"

Near begging.

But the man with the machine gun pointed behind Christie, back to where there had been a line of cars.

And when Christie turned, she saw another car from that line now racing toward them.

"Doc's coming. You can talk to him." The man nodded. "He'll decide what happens."

And Christie turned and watched as this other car raced toward them.

30
The Caravan

The new car pulling up was a compact—a steel-gray Civic, two doors, tiny compared to the big black SUV that had stopped them.

No one said anything as the car pulled close and stopped, with Christie and her car now sandwiched between the vehicles.

She looked at Kate, then Simon, forcing a smile.

Though she imagined her kids might be beyond reassurance.

Then, back to the car that had just stopped as a man got out.

Full beard, sandy-brown hair, long. Denim shirt, sleeves rolled up. Jeans dotted with oil, grease… something black.

Though a lot of things could look black when they dried.

The man looked up at the sky, then to Christie.

He also turned to her kids and nodded as he smiled.

Then, sounding nearly ridiculous, "Hi."

Christie shook her head.

"You mind telling me… us… what you and your…" She looked back to the men with the guns behind her. "…men are doing? Why you stopped us?"

She had guessed he was a leader of the group.

The man scratched the back of his neck and nodded. "Sure. But think, maybe, your kids could put their weapons down?"

Christie looked at the man.

"And your men, they will put theirs down as well?"

As soon as she said that, she realized how crazy that must sound.

What is she doing?

Having a standoff with her kids in the front lines?

"For their safety. For ours. Maybe…" Another smile… "…just lower them."

Christie turned to Kate and Simon and nodded. And they both pointed their guns to the ground.

"Great. Now to your question…"

The man took a step toward Christie.

"First things first. I'm Sam Collier. Kinda leading this caravan here." He gave a nod back to the line of cars that had created a roadblock.

"Not sure why. But, anyway, I'm in charge."

"Caravan?"

He nodded. "Yeah. And we seem to be heading the same direction as you. Maybe… for the same reason?"

"We heard—someone told me—that there were people who had moved out to the Midwest. Michigan. That they had come together, figured how to make things better, get things to grow. Turn things around."

Another smile from the man, and Christie noticed that his smile was laced with sadness.

And Christie had to wonder, *Are we all chasing a myth?*

Like the Flying Dutchman?

Doing all that travel, taking all those chances for…

There was a word she taught when covering Greek and Roman mythology with her mostly disinterested students.

A chimera.

"Heard the same thing. Though more than just heard."

The man looked right at Christie, and she had the feeling he was about to tell her something, but then he had first weighed the advisability of sharing it.

"I worked on this team. Researchers. CDC. Like a lot of teams.

Trying to learn what we could. At first, about the human cannibals—"

"The Can Heads," Christie said.

"Yes. If that's what we must call them. But then, despite the drought, despite the changes in climate, what really made so many crops fail? Why did so many plants die, as if whatever once drove their growth had suddenly ended?"

"Doc," a voice said from behind, "we best get moving."

The man talking to Christie nodded.

"Yeah. Look. Not the place for a history lecture here."

"Why did you stop us?"

"We didn't know how you were, why you were on this road. Maybe following us? Maybe tracking us?"

"We're alone," Christie said. "Obviously."

"I see. Look, we're very cautious. Always watching. Who's behind us, who's in front. What we're heading into. But now that you're here..."

He looked at her kids and Ben standing there looking—a gentle giant beside them.

Doubt he understands too much of what's going on here, she thought.

"Why not join us? Probably heading to the same place and—"

"Doc."

Again the voice form a one of the men behind Christie who— she reminded herself—all held powerful guns. "Things like that the group needs to vote on."

Again Sam Collier, "Doc"—*a scientist*—scratched his head. "I know, I know. We'll vote. Um, for now, they can come. I'm sure the group will be okay with it, Rob. We can save the vote for later."

A pause, no one saying anything, and Christie guessed that everything didn't always go smoothly in this travelling band.

"So join us. For now?"

He made a side-long glance at her kids as if messaging, *Think of them.*

And Christie could face the obvious.

Better chance of surviving, of getting there—if they worked with others.

Not a lot different from the days of the Oregon Trail, she thought.

"And this caravan... it has rules?"

"Can tell you all that later. Not a lot." Then he turned to the men with the guns. "After the vote."

And Christie thought a second.

So hard to tell these days what was a good decision, a bad one—and what could be a fatal one.

In fact, are there any good decisions at all?

"Okay," she said. "At least for tonight."

And Sam smiled. "Good. Now, we've been stopped here for a while, You got gas supplies... food?"

She nodded.

"Great. Then we'd best get going. Still a lot of miles to cover."

And the leader walked back to his car.

And without knowing much more than she and these people had a common goal, and that they were cautious, even guarded, Christie felt relief as he pulled away.

The men with guns got back into their big SUV, and Christie walked back to her car, giving the kids what she thought was a hopeful smile.

"Okay, kids, let's go."

And she braced herself for what she thought would be a lot of questioning from the kids, once the doors were shut and they joined the long caravan of cars heading west.

But the flood of questions didn't come.

Somehow, the kids maybe picked up on Christie's flicker of trust in the man they called "Doc."

Or, maybe the idea of not alone after so many days of running, all on their own, had taken its toll.

Kate did have a few pointed questions.

"Mom, what do you think the rules will be?"

"Not sure, Kate."

All of that standing had caused the pain in Christie's leg to flare up, and driving was becoming difficult.

She'd have to let Kate take over again soon.

"They *can't* have our guns," Kate said.

Christie nodded. "Right."

"Or our food," Simon added. "We found it. It's ours."

"That too, Simon."

Nothing for a few moments, then Kate, "It can't be like that other place. They had us trapped there."

When Christie had gotten into the car, she again checked that her gun was firmly nestled between the driver's seat and the door.

None of what the kids feared would be allowed to happen. One way or the other, she thought.

She saw Ben, sitting in the back.

He was looking out the window as Christie drove close to the line of cars, falling into line behind a silvery, beat-up Toyota that had lost all it hubcaps.

The caravan began moving.

But Ben's face, normally so open, at ease, now seemed troubled, brow furrowed, eyes narrowed.

"Ben," she said. "You okay?"

He turned and looked into the rear view mirror, his eyes on hers.

"Yes, Mrs.... Christie. It's just that..."

He hesitated.

"...I don't *know* these people."

Christie smiled. This giant of a man needed reassurance as well.

"Neither do I, Ben. All strangers. But what they're doing, travelling together, watching out for each other, it makes sense."

She looked away from the road, the cars ahead, to look right into his eyes. "That make sense to you?"

It took a few seconds. But then Ben nodded. "Sure."

Then, less sure... "Guess so."

Which is when Simon did an amazing thing...

He patted Ben's right shoulder, a massive thing, a football player's shoulder.

"Ben, we're together. If it's not a good thing, we'll *all* know. And we won't stay."

And that made the man smile.

He had to have been on his own for such a long time, she knew.

Must be amazing to now be part of this... family.

*

And the caravan rolled on, at a slow steady pace, stopping only to allow cars to refuel with their tanks, some people looking back at Christie's car, her family, this new addition, as the sun started to edge closer to the horizon.

And night began to fall.

31
We Stop at Night

The caravan pulled off the highway, with the sun still above the horizon but night close.

Christie slowed down. She couldn't wait to get out of the driver's seat, to stretch her wounded leg out.

This can't be good for the stitches, the healing, she thought.

Tomorrow, Kate would drive.

Apparently one of the cars had gone ahead and found a place for them to stop for the night.

And now the row of cars wound its way off the highway, to a two-lane blacktop road that seemed to lead nowhere.

Barren fields on either side, still in the grips of a winter chill, though spring—and whatever that would bring—was only weeks away.

And the evening seemed almost balmy. Christie had her window down.

The air cool, but refreshing, and when the road veered to the left, she was driving with the low-hanging sun right in her eyes.

In a few minutes, the lead cars pulled off the road onto a dirt driveway.

To a farmhouse. A barn. And a field.

Back in the day they grew corn here. Maybe had livestock, chickens?

Now deserted. Farms like this had vanished everywhere.

The cars stopped, and someone from the lead car, a middle-aged woman in jeans, with frizzy black hair speckled with gray, came back to her.

Christie saw she held what looked like an old-fashioned walkie-talkie in her hand.

"We're going to make our circle here," she said.

"Circle?"

"Just, um, do what I do."

The woman then hurried back to her car.

"We're staying here tonight?" Simon asked.

"Yes. Looks that way."

"In that house?" Kate asked. "Or the barn?"

Kate didn't sound thrilled.

But then Ben said, "I've never slept in a barn."

And everyone laughed.

The line began moving again, the circle beginning to form.

The cars formed a circle tight against the farmhouse and barn.

When Christie had stopped, leaving a couple of yards between her and the car in front, the same woman got out and gestured to her to come closer, make the circle tighter.

Christie nodded.

And then finally she could shut off the engine, dying to get out. As painful as walking could be, it would be so much better than sitting here.

Simon beat her to getting outside.

There were other kids here.

And those kids looked at Simon. Some older boys. A girl that looked near his age. Even a toddler, stumbling around.

As Christie popped her door and got out, she saw a young mother with a baby.

A baby.

Such a sign of hope, she thought. A future.

That's what a baby was, even when the world was falling apart.

Must have always been that way.

Kate came up to her. "Where we sleeping, Mom?"

Christie looked around for Sam—the man they called "Doc". She spotted him at one end of the circle, talking to people with rifles as he pointed left and then right.

"Not sure, Kate. I'll find out. Maybe the house. Maybe the barn." She took a breath. "If we have to, maybe the car."

Kate rolled her eyes at that.

Admittedly, the four of them sandwiched into the car didn't sound too appealing.

And they all knew how loudly Ben snored!

And funny. It was good to see a little of the old Kate just then, as if her daughter for a moment felt that she didn't always have to be so strong, always holding things together.

Just a bit of teenage girl there.

And that—like the baby—also represented hope.

"Okay to explore a bit?" Simon asked. "Just walk around?"

Christie looked at the tight circle of cars. The people that Sam had been talking to began to walk to different spots in the circle.

A few other people began stacking a pile of wood in the center of the circle. Mostly some splintery fence posts, but then Christie saw chunks of furniture being dragged out of the house.

A rocking chair. A bookcase. Some straight-backed kitchen chairs.

The sun nearly down, and in a minute, someone set fire to all that wood.

"Sure," she said. "Just stay inside the circle. We can eat some food in a bit."

She forced a smile.

"Okay?"

Simon nodded, and with his new guardian in tow—the lumbering Ben like his special giant—Simon started walking around the circle.

Been a while since he's been with other kids, Christie thought.

And that was something she knew he liked.

To explore, to play.

To get into trouble.

"How about you, Kate?"

"I'll take a walk too." Then she added pointedly, Kate's guard never even getting close to being let down. "Take a look at everyone."

Christie nodded.

And then she was alone, the people with rifles positioning themselves around the circle, the fire now growing.

Way more than a campfire, massive, and with the barn and house part of that circle... more wood close by, posts, planks.

After all, tomorrow they'd just move on.

And when the sun finally slipped below the horizon, she started walking to the warmth, to the glow of that great fire.

*

Someone touched her elbow.

She turned to see Sam, standing there, warm smile on his face.

"Settling in?"

Christie looked around the circle of cars.

"I used to teach history. You steal this idea from the settlers heading west?"

Sam looked away, grinning, then back to Christie. "It worked for them. We keep guards all night on the perimeter, in shifts."

"'Circle the wagons.'"

"Why, reckon that's the i-dea, ma'am."

And Christie laughed at that, thinking, *Been a while since I laughed.*

She saw a car outside the circle though—a dark maroon, with giant fins, backlit by the glow from the setting sun.

"That car, not in the circle, is there...?"

Sam looked at the direction she pointed. "Oh, right. Well, when we travel we're always scouting—another wild-west technique I guess!—in front and in back. And that... is our fastest car."

"What's it going to do?"

"Do just that—scout. Different teams take it out. It's what they used to call—in the day—a muscle car. Real fast. Any trouble ahead for the morning—"

"Or in the night—"

"Yeah, that too. Well, it comes back, tells me, the other people."

"Smart idea."

Christie watched the car pull away, racing down the dirt road, vanishing into the darkness until just its twin headlights could be seen winding away.

Then she turned back to Sam.

"Mind if we sit? It's hard on my leg."

The man nodded. "Sure. There are some stumps by the fire. Nice night. What happened? Something bad? To your leg?"

Christie nodded. "Something? Could say that…"

And she walked along with him to the giant fire shooting glowing yellow spikes into the sky.

*

After Christie had told him what happened to her leg, Sam asked where they had come from.

And the big question…

Why were they on their own?

Christie hesitated for a moment.

So much to tell. Their history. All the terrible things. And Jack's sacrifice that saved them all.

How they had all changed.

And though she felt like she didn't want to talk about any of it, somehow the man's voice—the way he asked a question, then let silence sit there for a moment—made Christie tell it all.

Fast as she could.

Not dwelling on any moment more terrible than the other.

Thinking she was holding it together.

But when she finished, she was crying, tears running down her cheeks despite how quickly she dabbed at her eyes with her sleeve.

For a moment she thought Sam would put an arm around her.

And that, she knew, would only make it worse.

Instead—in a quiet, steady way—he just sat there.

And when her tears stopped, and she took a big breath, ready to move on as the tear trails dried on her cheek, he said, "You have been through so much."

The obvious.

But it was enough for her to turn to him, a sad smile on her face, "Why yes I have."

Then, "One thing I can tell you. I talked to the others. If you want... you can stay with us. Move along with us. You won't be alone."

"Really? Everyone here okay with that?"

And now Sam laughed.

"Not everyone. Pretty—um—diverse group. But you got the votes. People here still have a heart. Most of them, anyway."

Then, quietly, "Thanks."

"Now you just need to decide."

"Stay... or go?"

Christie looked at the man's eyes. She knew nearly nothing about him, but she felt safer—even supported—sitting here with him.

She saw Simon over with other kids.

Kids with kids.

Good to see that.

And Kate? She seemed to have found a girl near her age.

The two of them nearly women.

But Christie had to remind herself, *My daughter is still growing. She isn't a woman.*

Not yet.

She needs this as much as Simon.

And maybe I do as well.

"I need to talk to my kids. But I think they will want to stay. Ben good to stay as well?"

She had nearly forgotten about him.

"Sure. Sweet guy. Looks strong. We could use that."

Christie nodded.

It seemed decided.

Then, "And what about you, Sam. Or 'Doc.' Your story? I mean, you don't have to, but—"

And her question made the man look away. His beard glowed with a reddish tinge from the fire.

And in what seemed his pattern, he took a few minutes before returning to Christie, to her question.

And probably hoping to race through it, to summarize it just as she did.

He began.

His voice low.

The tale, like for all of us, Christie thought, *so hard to tell*.

32
Of Hope and Michigan

"Doc? Well, we could actually use a real 'doc'. Me. I'm just a research scientist."

"*Just*..."

Sam smiled at that. "Molecular Biology. Worked for the government. Back... in the day. The Tharp Center, near Princeton."

Then it hit Christie.

This man sitting here, by the fire, might actually be one of those people who knew what happened.

Whatever it was that changed the world forever.

"You were studying this? The drought, the crops dying, the Can Heads..."

"Our team was. All of it. Thinking there had to be an explanation. And it had to be biological. Some genetic mutation. We had so many tests, studies going—you name it. And other places all around the country, same thing."

"And what did you find?"

At that question Sam paused. He looked away, his eyes catching the flickering flames of the bonfire.

"Not enough. And not fast enough. Lot of scientists were ready to jump on GMOs—"

"GMOs?"

"Genetically Modified Organisms. They altered foods that made tomatoes stay fresh and red, or could keep corn for weeks, or make apples resistant to insects."

"We were doing that?"

"Here, in the US… yes. Most countries, to some extent. But no matter. Once a GMO organism was created, all you needed was a stiff breeze and it was on the move."

"So is that what happened?"

"We weren't sure. Not yet, anyway. I was working on the other issue mostly… the Can Heads. But we shared everything, and it seemed that some of those altered genes could mutate on their own… like throwing a switch and one mutated gene could trigger another. Like dominos."

"More like a science fiction movie…"

Sam turned to her, and smiled.

"Exactly what we thought. A very scary movie. Thinking we're in control, and suddenly… we're not."

"And the Can Heads?"

Christie didn't even like saying the words. As if that only made them more real.

"We guessed they were linked… to the food crisis. And my team actually made a breakthrough, a bit of one."

"What was that?"

"We found out why some people turned, and others didn't. Again, it came down to genes. A level of genetic protection some people had… that others didn't. Probably linked to the plant mutations that had fully invaded the food chain. But we were years…"

He took a breath.

"…maybe *decades* away from finding the link. From changing things."

Christie nodded.

Then there was the obvious question.

One that she thought that perhaps she should be more cautious about asking.

"And how did you come here, Sam? Leading these people? Heading west."

And then... silence.

Sam's hand went to his beard. A scratch. Then, as if a speck of dust had drifted into an eye, he rubbed the socket with a knuckle.

And Christie so wished she hadn't asked that question.

"Plans... plans were being made. Where we lived and worked were—like a lot of places—getting more dangerous, electric fences or no fences. One group thought that—with time—they could undo some of the genetic alterations affecting food. They believed they could reengineer them... if they had the time and the space."

He took a breath. "They were going to head west."

"To Michigan?"

Sam nodded. "Reports came to us that Can Head activity in parts on the Michigan northeast coast, along Lake Huron, was less intense. Even heard that the drought hadn't been so severe, and the soil could still be good—or as good as we could get. A water supply... better than most places. And they had located a spot, a good defensible location that someone knew well. A place called Bald Mountain. Beautiful valley that led to the lake."

"They left first?"

"Right. The first caravan. Sending reports, while the rest of us rushed to get ready, last minute things, packing up, getting... getting as much food, gas..."

He stopped.

She knew what he was going to say.

And there was nothing she could do about it.

"Then one night..."

How many of us, Christie thought, *could tell such a story, beginning exactly the same way... "then one night..."*

"No advance warning. They came. Broke in somehow. Dozens of them. Like they had planned it, acting together."

And Jack had felt the same thing. That somehow the animal-like Can Heads could act together, like a pack.

"All the gunfire, so much shooting, the bodies piling up—but with so many. My wife, baby. Down in the basement. Safe. While I tried to deal with it."

He turned and looked at her.

Anyone who would be on this road would have a story.

Of loss. Love. Death.

"A back window. Boarded up. But a bunch had broken through. Couldn't even hear it above all the gunfire on the street, in the house. And I couldn't... couldn't..."

He stopped.

And Christie leaned across.

Touched his forearm.

She didn't say the obvious.

The thing that held absolutely no meaning here.

Those words absurd.

It's okay.

Instead, she just patted his arm while finally Sam lowered his head, and soundlessly covered his eyes with both his hands, his sob silent.

But with Christie's arm there, she felt his shaking, heaving.

And she just held that position—looking at him, looking at the fire—until it stopped.

When it ended, Sam turned, once again a smile on his face, though his eyes still glistened.

"Time you went in—the house, the barn. Your choice. Get some sleep?"

Christie nodded. She could still see her kids, still talking.

Like this was a campout. A big bonfire. All they needed were the marshmallows.

She stood up. "And tomorrow we get to Michigan..."

Sam stood as well. Nodded. "Hopefully. Sometimes reminds me of that song..."

"Hmm?"

"*Michigan seems like a dream to me now...*"

And Christie could easily finish the verse, the music suddenly there, in her brain.

All gone to look for America…

And she followed Sam as people took positions at the cars, guns ready, and others streamed into the farmhouse.

Undisturbed sleep would be good.

Even lying on the floor.

No matter.

Be good for her kids.

That's what she hoped was ahead.

But she couldn't have been more wrong.

kate

A mother's love for her child is like nothing else in the world. It knows no law, no pity, it dares all things and crushes down remorselessly all that stands in its path.
- Agatha Christie

33
The Innocent

Some of the people had headed to the barn, dragging pillows, blankets, anything to keep warm and sleep on.

Little kids dragged stuffed animals, the scene both beautiful and heartbreaking at the same time.

Christie had said to her kids to find a spot to sleep in the big farmhouse.

After the previous night, they'd both be so tired that they could likely sleep anywhere.

Christie's leg had begun to ache.

When a bathroom became empty—a room that had a long line from early on until well into the night—Christie went in, and with the antibiotic ointment and clean bandages in her hand, she unwrapped the wound to see the damage.

And despite the wound looking like cracked pavement, even glistening in spots, she could see that the wound did look like it was healing.

Some of the pain she was feeling was just that healing—skin scabbing, then being stretched.

Tomorrow Kate would drive... and she'd just let the leg get better.

Now, she rolled up the stained, dark maroon blood-stained

bandage and then spread the antibiotic ointment over the wound. Then, she wrapped it tight with a new bandage and used a metal clip to hold it into place.

Someone knocked at the door.

She had been in here for a while.

"Sorry," she said.

And then putting her jeans back on, she went to the door and opened it.

An old man with narrow eyes waited at the door.

No friendly smile here.

No matter what was happening in the world, Christie thought, *no one liked waiting for the bathroom.*

She gave the man a small smile and then hobbling past him. She went and looked for a place to lie down.

Shut her eyes.

Blessed sleep.

People on guard outside.

About as safe as they could be.

*

Her sleep had come fast, deep.

Crazy dreams swirled around. Memories of times in their backyard on Staten Island.

Then she... Jack... making love.

That dream so painful.

Feeling so real.

Then she walked through a world where the Can Heads were everywhere... but yet it seemed normal.

Can Heads pumping gas! Operating a checkout at the A&P.

As if the war was over, and they had won.

Terrifying—and yet funny at the same time.

Then, in the midst of that dream, she heard voices. The deep rumble of male voices. Then a woman, shrill, rising above that sound.

Not a dream.

Somewhere downstairs.

And Christie opened her eyes.

*

And when the loud voices continued, she struggled to stand up, then walk downstairs.

Something was going on.

And if there was one thing Christie knew, you just didn't keep your eyes closed in this world.

You just didn't turn over, and ignore things.

This wasn't a world where you could afford to be unconcerned.

And as she neared the bottom of the farmhouse's staircase...

She saw a bunch of men, rifles in hand. Sam there as well. And a few women, most older than Christie, but they too held guns.

Other people who had been sleeping sprawled on the living room floor—a few kids, and older people—remained on the floor, sitting, listening.

She didn't see Kate or Simon.

Good. Hopefully they could stay asleep.

Sam had noticed her on the stairs.

"What's happening?" Christie said.

Sam nodded, as if weighing how to respond.

He took steps toward Christie.

"One of the men scouting... running ahead of the road for tomorrow. Found something. Something we knew we might find."

Sam looked back at the circle of men and women, coats on. All ready to leave, go somewhere.

"What did they find?"

"These people. Heading west as well. But—"

Now the man who had first stopped Christie just that day walked over. "We gotta go, Doc. Now's the time."

Christie kept her eyes on Sam.

Christie realized she asked the next question so quietly, "What kind of people?"

"You know what you saw, what almost happened to your son?"

She shook her head. "No…"

"Keeping…" Sam struggled to say the words. "…children, kids in a pen, travelling with them…"

He left the rest unfinished.

There were kids in the room.

Christie thought, *unfinished is best.*

"What are you going to do?"

Sam took a breath. A glance at the people behind him, guns ready. Faces grim.

"We're going to get them."

Yes, Christie realized, *that's what has to happen.*

Must happen.

"I'll help. I'll go too."

Sam was quick to shake his head. "No. I mean, we can use all the help we can get. But with your leg—"

"I can still shoot, even drive."

"You could be a liability to us."

And as soon as he said it, she knew he was right.

A trip, a stumble, and she could turn into a prisoner, someone else they'd have to rescue… along with all those kids.

She nodded in agreement.

Which is when she heard a familiar voice, just behind her.

The voice steady, strong, determined. "I'll go."

Christie turned and looked at Kate, standing just feet from the stairs.

Gun in hand.

She was ready to say, *What are you talking about?*

You'll go to this… place? Where these men, these monsters are keeping kids?

Kids…

Prisoners. Travelling with them.

For food.

But Sam beat her to it.

He walked over to Kate, looked down at her gun.

"Kate, thanks for offering. But best you stay here."

And then Christie saw Kate took a step closer to the cluster of people, mostly men, but two women also standing with them.

Kate looked at her, then around at the others.

"I've shot people—like these people. I saved my brother. If I can help save others, then that's what I should do."

Sam looked over at Christie as if asking for some help here.

But then Christie realized: Her Kate from long ago, her little girl, was gone. Kate had saved Simon, then she saved her, dragging her out of that mountain house, carrying a weight that should have crushed her.

Christie realized, that in this world, Kate should go.

"We don't know how many people are there, what kind of weapons, just that they're there."

"More the reason I should go."

One thing about Kate: When she got an idea, she got an idea.

"Besides, all those kids. They'll be scared. Could even get hurt as you try to free them. I could help with that."

Ideas. And logic.

And Christie turned to Sam.

"Sam, I love my daughter; I don't want her to go. But she's right. I wouldn't be here but for her. I can't go…"

A look back at Kate.

"But she *can*."

Sam scratched his head. He obviously would like every gun he could. And he also needed to have people stay here so there was some defense of the wagon-train circle of cars.

Then, he nodded.

"Okay. But we all—"

And then from somewhere in the kitchen, out lumbered the giant figure of Ben.

"I'll go too."

Sam did an eye roll. He probably thought Ben was big, strong…

but maybe… also a liability?

"I can help you too," Ben said.

It looked like Sam was about to draw the line at Ben joining the raid, which is when Christie leaned close to Sam, lowered her voice.

"He twisted a Can Head's… head off. With just his bare hands. Think you should take him."

Sam grinned at that.

"Okay. Everyone buddy up in cars."

Then quickly before there could be any more debate, "And Kate, Ben… you come with me. Rob, bring up the rear, all right?"

Nods all around, and then people shuffled to the door of the farmhouse.

And among them, Kate.

Christie thinking that she shouldn't look back. But then—just at the door—she did turn back and smiled at her mother.

And Christie smiled back even though the only thing she really felt—could really feel right now—was fear.

34
The Raid

The cars were moving *so* slowly Kate thought.

Over winding, narrow roads, that gradually streamed past empty, still-frozen fields, and then on up, to hills.

"You okay?" the man said. Sam.

The leader—and her mother had told her—a scientist.

Though now, with his full beard and denim shirt, he looked more like a farmer, or some kind of mountain man.

Kate wasn't sure she liked him.

"I'm fine."

He nodded, smiled at that. Then to the man in the back seat.

"Ben, you all right?

"Just fine."

Then a question from Ben—almost funny.

So classic.

"We almost there yet?"

And Sam pointed to the hill.

"They are on the other side of that hill. Big house, property sits away from the woods. Least that's what one of my guys said. They're probably still there."

The line of cars moved on.

And with every bit of distance closer to that hill, now looking like a sleeping giant animal in the distance, Kate felt more tension.

She had volunteered to do this.

She didn't have to.

But she knew what was the right thing to do.

Even though—right now—it didn't feel that way at all.

Then, at the base of the hills ahead, Sam stopped.

And all the other cars pulled to a slow stop behind him.

He picked up the thing he talked on.

A walkie-talkie, whatever that was.

"Okay, everyone. We kill the lights here. Then we're going to go up the hill nice and slow. Then, we'll see what we're going to do."

Kate looked at Sam.

Didn't sound like much of a plan.

See what we're going to do?

But then, lights killed, Sam started his car again.

Kate looked behind, a smile to Ben, and then a look at the dark line of cars trailing behind them.

"Stay inside for now," Sam said, stopping the car at what appeared to be the top of a hill.

Kate nodded.

Sam held big binoculars as he got out of the car.

A few of the other drivers walked up to him.

Kate couldn't hear what they were saying—their breath making smoky clouds, so cold on top of this hill. But as her eyes adjusted to the dark, she could see them pointing and gesturing one way, then the other.

Ben asked a question. "Kate, are you scared?"

Kate thought about lying. Instead, she turned back to the man and nodded. "Sure. A little. But we gotta do this. Save their kids."

Ben nodded back. Then, "I'm scared too. But I want to help." He smiled, proud of his next statement. "I've always wanted to help. People always liked that about me."

"I'm sure they did, Ben. I know we do, Mom, me—"

"Simon too!" Ben said, his smile broadening.

"Especially Simon!" Kate said, laughing.

And her little talk with Ben made some of her fear go away.

Guess that's how it works, she thought.

Make someone else feel better, and well… you feel better.

Then the group of people outside broke up, heading back to their cars, as Sam got back in.

His eyes catching some of the light. Even with a beard she could tell that he looked concerned.

Or, maybe some fear there as well?

"All right."

He turned to her. "Let me tell you what we're going to do. And…" Now a bit of a smile. "…what *you're* going to do."

Kate nodded.

"You still remember how to drive, right?"

Another nod from Kate.

And she listened to what was supposed to happen in the minutes to come.

*

Kate drove slowly, right in the middle of the four cars that had pulled away from the people on the hill.

Sam had put Ben in one of the front cars, so she drove alone.

Alone, the car empty to make room for the children they were to rescue.

Kate gripped the steering wheel tightly. The lights were off, as with all the cars, but her eyes had adjusted to the darkness. A moon would help, but it would also help those who could spot them.

They were to drive down the hill, then follow a twisting two-lane road that circled behind the house.

Once there, they would wait.

While the others—men, women, loaded with guns—crept slowly closer, leaving their cars on the hill.

She had thought that would be so terrifying to do.

To abandon your car, in the night.

Walk through the brush and fields on foot, creeping down low, to surprise the people who held those kids captive.

And then—when the others attacked from the front—as soon as they heard the guns firing, they were to come close to the house.

To what looked like a small barn, a small building to the side where they had spotted the children being kept.

Lights on in the main house.

Voices carrying in the night.

Everyone well fed.

Her hands were locked on the steering wheel; her stomach tightened.

The thought of what those people did, so calmly, with such care, terrified her. It made her want to throw up.

It's why she asked to do this.

Her mother couldn't.

But she could.

The line of cars reached the winding country road.

They would get close.

Then stop, windows open, the chilly night air snaking in.

Engines killed.

And wait.

*

It seemed to take forever.

Sitting there, listening for the sound of the guns.

Then the woman who drove the lead car—her face etched with lines, hair frizzy, flying in all directions—came back to the cars one by one.

When she got to Kate...

"You okay?"

Kate nodded.

The woman nodded back.

Is she afraid as well? Kate wondered.

"Soon as we hear the guns, we start up again. Not too close. Just enough so we can get to that building. There will be guards there, I guess. But they'll be distracted. We need to shoot them." She looked down at Kate's rifle on the seat beside her. "You can shoot, hit things?"

Kate had to clear her throat to answer. "Yes. I can."

"Good. Make every bullet count. Then…"

The woman looked away, cocking an ear.

Nothing yet.

"…then we get in there. The kids will be scared. Really scared. Some of them will know what's been happening. They'll think we're just like them. They'll be so frightened they may fight back."

Kate nodded. "I-I can try to…" She searched for the word. "…calm them."

Only then did the woman smile.

"Good. That's why it's a good thing you're here." A pause. "Almost a kid yourself."

Kate nodded.

She felt anything but a kid.

The woman started for the other cars behind Kate.

While Kate—shivering in the seat, her right hand now resting on her gun, as if they could provide some security—waited.

Then the gunfire.

So sudden, exploding out of nowhere.

To her left, Kate saw the brilliant sparks, the flashes from the guns.

She also forgot to start her car until the car in front of her had resumed its slow creep along the highway, through the darkness.

And with the window rolled up, she could still hear the guns blasting.

This is what a war must sound like, she thought.

Sam, the others, attacking the front of the building.

Would Ben—so, so gentle—be okay, trying to help but with all that gunfire terrifying him?

Kate also had to wonder, *Would that be enough to distract the guards who watched the kids, guarding them like they were animals?*

She would know soon enough.

35
The Rescue

Christie leaned across the hood of the gray Toyota Camry, rifle pointed out to the darkness.

She had said she could do a watch. A few hours on guard, at the circle of cars.

One of the men, older, a bit wobbly in his walk as well, had said that wasn't necessary.

But in truth, Christie couldn't imagine going to sleep until her daughter came back.

She was so proud of her—how she came forward, and insisted that she go.

And Christie knew there was no way she could, or should, stop her.

But now, this waiting… It was terrible.

At least Simon was sleeping.

Or she hoped he was.

They were all so sleep deprived, but she thought that she was starting to see signs that all this was changing Simon, hurting him.

The way he'd gaze off, as if lost in thought, then come back.

He needed sleep.

The woman next to her, again older, left behind to make room for the kids they would be rescuing tonight.

But also left behind to stand watch, keeping the circle safe.

She had positioned herself next to Christie.

"Feeling scared?" the woman said.

"Now? Sure. Haven't felt safe in a while."

The woman, who had been one of the few to stick out a hand and introduce herself—"*Name's Anna Devoe*"—nodded. "Any stray Can Heads come this way and we can handle them."

There seemed to be a lot of people on guard around the circle. And as soon as the raiding party came back, they could divide the watch into shifts.

Christie so wanted to sleep so badly.

Just as soon as she knew Kate was safe.

"But what about, you know... your daughter?"

Christie turned and looked at the woman.

Christie would have rather not talked about that at all. But then she realized that there might be some wisdom, some compassion, in the old woman's question.

Rather than just have the torturous, worried thoughts, maybe it would be better to talk about it.

"Yeah. I'm scared."

"Makes sense. My kid, I'd worry too."

Christie wondered if this woman had children.

Or did she have children and lose them?

"That girl of yours... seems strong."

"She is. Been through a lot. Simon and I wouldn't be here if not for her."

Then the old woman looked away.

"Then she'll be fine. Be good for the kids those animals keep to see her young face." She took a breath. "Real good."

Christie nodded in the darkness.

And then her mind went back to what was happening, right now, miles away.

And she could only imagine...

*

The line of cars came only a little closer to the dark building where the children might be kept imprisoned.

How must the kids be reacting to the gunfire?

Would they know it represented hope, or just more terror in their lives?

Kate saw the other people getting out, crouching low as they formed a line, scuttling toward the house, the small barn, the gunfire now before them.

Just never stopping...

Kate followed along, crouched down as well, though she thought that anyone who looked this way would easily spot them, this funny line of people streaming to the back of the garage.

As they got closer, the woman in front held up a hand.

They stopped, and Kate saw the woman standing there, just looking at the back of the building.

And Kate could see what the woman saw.

No way in through the back.

They'd have to go around the front.

And there would be people there, even with all the shooting out by the main house. They must have a guard there.

Maybe more than one.

But the line kept moving, and Kate with it.

*

Christie looked up to the sky.

Still middle of the night, but she saw a slight glow to the east.

Too early for dawn. A sliver of a moon about to rise?

That would be good, she thought. *Could see better.*

And again, her mind drifted to her daughter, as she thought really only one thing.

Hurry. Come back fast.

And then realizing what she was really thinking...

Come back.

*

The woman in front stopped again. A quick look to all those behind her.

In the darkness, she raised a hand, and Kate could barely make out what she was doing.

Three fingers extended.

Then she made the hand spin in the air.

Then two fingers.

Counting down.

Then a last finger.

Kate gripped her rifle tighter, moving her finger into the circle made by the trigger.

Her other hand confirming that the safety was off.

It felt like her heart was racing, that it might explode.

The woman's arm went down, and now everyone in the line surged forward, their slow crouch gone as they ran, full out, around to the front.

As soon as Kate hit the corner of the building, she heard a blast, and a man standing in front of the garage doors fell forward, blood dripping from his mouth.

Other people turned to face the main house.

Because people would come from there now, even though they were under attack from the front.

These... *people*... would act to protect their "food."

For a moment, Kate froze, and then she raced forward to the woman and a young man standing near her by the garage doors.

The two of them rattled a chain.

A bunch of padlocks snapped tight on the links, keeping the barn sealed.

"What can I do?" Kate said.

She looked over her shoulder. Then to the other men and women in their group who had all knelt down, guns pointed to where the firefight continued to rage.

"Have to be fast. We get in there, they'll be scared and..."

Kate nodded. "I'll help get them. Tell them it's okay."

Then she saw the woman point her rifle barrel at the coil of locks and chain.

A blast, chain breaking up but still one link held fast, and a second lock intact.

"They're coming. Some of them coming this way," one of the kneeling people said.

But the woman simply moved her rifle in a different direction, taking care that it pointed down at the other lock, to the ground, and not into the building itself.

Another blast.

The kids inside—they must be terrified, Kate thought.

And now the man, not much older than Kate really, more of a boy, pulled at the freed chain, pulling its pieces through the latches that held the garage tight,

Behind her, Kate heard constant firing from the people kneeling.

They'd have to keep the people away while they freed the kids.

The garage doors flew open.

And Kate raced in first.

She saw nothing. The smell of hay. Other, foul smells. Maybe from animals that used to live in here. The place so dark.

But as her eyes adjusted to the even inkier darkness inside, she could see something.

Shapes standing in the back.

Huddled. Almost invisible.

And despite the noise of the gunfire outside, Kate said—trying to make her voice and steady and strong as she could—"It's okay. We're here to help you. We're here to get you away."

The line of shapes—maybe six, seven, eight, all different heights—none of them moved.

So Kate walked over to them.

With a few steps she saw eyes in that darkness, catching whatever little light there was.

The eyes all locked on her.

And Kate hoped that they could see her face a bit.

Because she smiled.

She smiled, and said, "We have to hurry. Before they come. You're safe now."

She kept the smile on. "But we have to go now."

Then so slowly, so it would appear to be a gentle gesture, she extended her hand.

Thinking, hoping, that one of them would take it.

Please, she thought. *Take my hand.*

Nothing. No movement.

And then from the dark line of figurers, the terrified children standing, their backs to the corner of the barn, a single hand reached out.

Kate gently closed on it.

Then, she saw the woman behind her, letting her do this, and she whispered, "Everyone follow me. Fast as we can. Okay?"

Did any heads bob "yes?"

She couldn't tell.

All she could tell was that when she turned to leave this foul smelling barn, this prison for children, the gunfire seemed like it was now constant.

She had to just keep moving, holding a little kid's hand who had been brave enough to take hers.

In the other, her gun, which she might still need, she knew.

They were far from safety out of here.

And Kate moved the line of kids out of the darkness of the barn's corners, to the open door, to the mayhem of the guns outside, to the night.

And—she hoped—*to escape.*

36
They're Coming

Christie yawned. There was no one to take her place, not without waking kids like Simon, and the few really old, almost infirm, people.

And they all needed sleep so badly.

The woman next to her, Anna, at once fell asleep.

And Christie let her have ten minutes before she gave her a gentle nudge and the woman awoke.

"Must've dozed off," the woman said.

"It happens," Christie said, smiling.

Wouldn't mind doing that myself, she thought.

Ten minutes.

Five minutes.

Even one minute. Shut my eyes.

That would be so precious.

But soon the raiding party would be back.

Kate, those kids.

They could take turns guarding the circle.

Soon, she thought. *Has to be soon.*

But then she saw something out in the black wilderness that stretched from the circle of cars, off to a thick woods of mostly barren trees, but with some conifers looking tall and dark, shadowy in the night.

Headlights. Heading this way.

Instinctively, Christie straightened up.

*

Kate gave the small hand held in hers a little squeeze.

And even though she heard bullets ripping into the wooden planks behind her, she paused to turn to the kids.

Not a line now, still bunched together, but hands locked, a human web of clenched hands, their faces looking empty, eyes wide.

"We're going to—"

A bunch of bullets flew what felt like inches from Kate's head, splintering more of the wood boards behind her.

"—crouch down, like this..."

Kate demonstrated.

The woman who had led them in was at the back, tapping kids, pointing down to the ground to get them to get as low as they could.

"Now, fast!" Kate said.

And she had to pull the hand she held *hard*, hoping that with all those interlocked hands, the group of kids would just get pulled along.

She hit the corner of the building and quickly ran to the back, turning to where the cars were.

For a moment, she couldn't tell where the cars were. Everything looked different in the darkness.

Were they just ahead, or did she have to cut a bit to the right?

She had slowed, and a few of the kids had actually bumped into her, like toys on wheels that kept rolling even when she stopped.

A moment's hesitation.

"Keep moving," the woman at the back of the kids said.

Kate thought she saw the path they took just to the right.

And Kate started running again.

And even as she did, she thought she heard the gunfire, now...

What was the word?

Sporadic.

No longer constant.

And they weren't even at the cars yet, and with just this one woman helping her herd the kids, Kate thought, *That could be either a good thing... or a very bad thing.*

*

The car in the dark raced wildly over the empty road, looking like a crazed beast on the narrow strip of pavement that led to the house.

Why is it going so fast? Christie wondered.

It was one of those scout cars.

A fast car.

Now racing back here.

For a moment she didn't have a clue. It seemed so odd.

Then... she did.

*

Appearing out of the darkness like mysterious shapes from another world, Kate saw the line of cars.

She glanced behind her. The woman urging the kids forward.

She wanted to ask the woman, *What about the others. Are they coming?*

We have to get out of here.

But Kate kept focused on moving forward until she got to the front car and released the hand she held.

And a small voice went, "No."

That small hand refusing to be freed.

Kate whispered, "We have to all get in. Bunch of you with me, the rest with..."

She realized that she didn't know the other woman's name.

An ally in this strange mission, this attack.

Nameless.

"Some of you come with me," the woman said.

And Kate watched the woman separating some of the hands and steering three of the kids to her car, farther to the rear, where the barren woods began.

Kate had five of them.

Sam had said, *Get the kids. Get back. Don't wait for anything, anyone.*

And that's what Kate did, the four doors of the car open as the kids scrambled in.

Then Kate got into the driver's seat.

"We okay?" she said. "Everyone all right?"

No one answered.

Kate started the car.

And with the doors shut, and the engine started, Kate realized she could smell the children.

How long had it been since they'd showered, washed, anything?

With gunfire still sounding all around, she turned the wheel of the car hard.

And now, driving to the road away from this place, she had to turn on the lights.

Hard to see where the damn road was.

She opened her window. Needed some air.

Thinking, *what's been done to these kids? What's happened to them.*

And as the car made its bumpy way over rocks and pits in the ground, she heard a small voice in the back.

Could have been any one of them.

The words so simple, so crazy...

"*Thank you.*"

*

Christie watched the red car rumble up to the circle as if it might smash its way through protective ring of cars.

But one of the men had gotten into a car, pulled it out of the way, and made an opening.

The scout car stormed through the opening, braked, sending up a dusty cloud of dirt visible even in the darkness.

Then the man—Rob—got out.

And one look at him, and Christie could tell he was way beyond scared.

A group had formed around him, gun barrels pointed down.

For the moment ignoring their defensive positions. No eyes looking out to the deeper darkness away from the farmhouse and barn.

All eyes on Rob, gasping for air.

Rob looked around at the group as if they didn't get it.

"What? They're not back yet? The others?"

One of the old men shook his head. "Should be soon. What's going on?"

Rob shook his head as if he couldn't believe what he was about to say. "They're coming. *Hundreds* of them. From back there, like an army. Can Heads, marching here."

Then he stopped, again taking in the circle of fifteen or so people who had been on guard.

Then he nodded, the truth in his next words so obvious.

"We have to wake everyone. *Now.* Get everyone up who can shoot. They were moving fast, coming together like they had a plan."

Christie thought of something Jack always said: *Can Heads can't plan.*

They're not like wolves.

Was that still true?

For a moment, nobody did anything, then he said, "Some of you, get back onto the circle; the rest, wake everyone the hell up now."

And Christie turned to Anna.

"I'm going to get my son…"

Christie could see that the older woman's eyes were glistening. She had been crying.

How much horror had she seen? How much more did she think she was about to see?

Tonight…

"You stay here. I'll be back with him. Okay?"

Just a nod.

And Christie ran as fast she could, joining the others.

To sound the alarm. Get everyone up.

And what she felt… as she ran… went way beyond any fear she had ever felt before.

37
The Stand

Kate hit one deep rut, and it sent her and her small passengers flying up to hit the ceiling of the car. The kids screamed.

"Sorry," she said.

Can't see anything, she thought, *even with the lights on.*

She looked in the mirror and saw the other car behind her, the nameless woman with three kids.

The total: eight.

Eight saved.

But how many had been lost before this?

And how much of *that... back there...* had these kids seen?

The human monsters selecting a kid, taking it away from the others.

Screaming. Kicking.

And then—in that moment of distraction—she saw two men ahead.

Right in front of the rocky path to the road, guns raised.

Kate's gun was beside her, on the floor of the car near the door.

No way she could manage steering the car and grabbing the gun and—

And with their guns raised, one of the men raised a hand signaling for her to halt.

But there was no way she would do that.

No way at all.

She yelled.

"Kids. Get down! Low as you can. On the floor. Do it!"

Making her voice as stern as possible.

She couldn't get her gun, and with two barrels aimed right at the car, the men figured she would have to stop.

Her attempt to rescue the children, to end the horror of their cannibalism, would be over.

But it was a situation where there was no choice about what to do.

No trees hugged the rocky path, just scrubby brush that scraped at the car's sides like fingers as it bounced past.

What Kate did next she didn't have any idea what it might do.

But she slammed her foot down hard on the accelerator.

She could hear the wheels instantly screaming, even with the windows shut.

In the mirror, she couldn't see any of the kids.

But she could hear them.

Their cries constant as now, in addition to making the car fly over the ruts so fast, she cut the steering wheel hard to the right, then to the left.

Even while she heard the shots blasting from the men's guns…

*

"Simon…" Christie said, her voice close to her son's right ear.

She could feel the warmth of his sleeping body, on the floor, but he had found a small, square throw pillow.

"Simon, you have to get up."

His eyes opened so slowly, reluctantly.

"Hmmm?" he said.

Christie forced a smile.

"Simon, we need to get everyone outside, Everyone who can…"

The words sounded absurd.

"…shoot. They think… some Can Heads are coming."

Keeping her smile on as she lied.

"Just want all the help we can get. Just in case."

But she thought she saw in Simon's eyes… an awareness.

That she wasn't telling the truth.

Smiles or no smiles.

And when he didn't move…

"Come on, Simon. We don't have a lot of time."

Those words betraying her fear.

But those words brought a nod.

The house had turned noisy, chaotic with the sound of others being awakened, the frenzied shouts of people grabbing guns, asking questions, of…

Panic.

That's what this is, Christie thought.

Simon stood up, yawned.

He grabbed his gun.

"Safety's…?" she started.

"On. Sure, Mom."

And he followed his mother, still looking half asleep, out to the cold morning light.

*

Kate jerked the car one way, then the other. She heard the kids rattle around both beside her and in the back.

And with one yank, she thought she'd send the car rolling over, spinning out of control.

But all the while doing these crazy turns, she heard the gunfire.

She heard one bullet crash into the back windshield, then another to a side window.

Then, she felt a thump.

Someone who had been trying to stop her had been hit, and hard.

She gripped the steering wheel so tightly her hand ached.

And now thinking that the other person shooting would now be behind her, she stopped the erratic turns and still—with her foot flat on the accelerator, all the way down—she steered the car straight down to the road.

"Stay down," she said loudly, just in case any of the screaming, crying kids were tempted to sit up.

The car rocketed toward the road.

And when she hit the pavement, she made a sharp a turn to get onto the road, and she thought she felt the car's right wheels fly off the ground.

The tires' screams matching the sounds from inside the car.

A quick glance to the mirror, the other car still behind her.

And Kate thought, *We're away.*

We did it.

We're safe!

*

Christie pulled the still sleepy Simon to the outer circle of cars, finding her spot next to the woman, Anna.

"Thought you might not come back," Anna said.

Christie smiled.

"My son's a good shot. Isn't that right, Simon?"

Simon nodded.

Then the woman asked a question that Christie wished she hadn't.

"How much ammunition do you have?"

Christie nodded.

"I have... what's in the rifle. Then nearly a full box. What is that?"

"Twenty," the woman said.

Okay. So that was how many shots Christie had.

"And your boy?"

Christie put a hand on his head.

"Simon?"

Then, like he was digging for some treasured toy, Simon stuck a hand into each pocket and pulled out shells.

"The gun's loaded," he said. "And I got..."

He counted.

He counted.

"Another ten... eleven."

The woman didn't say anything.

But now they all knew exactly how many times they could fire their weapons.

"See anything yet?" Christie asked.

"No. Looks like nothing out there."

Then Simon spoke, "Maybe they've gone somewhere else."

And not believing her words, Christie said, "Maybe."

Which is when someone standing on the back of a pickup truck yelled, "Here they come!"

The words cutting through the night.

Then, "Get ready. Everyone... get ready."

And before Christie turned to look at the approaching horde, she pulled Simon close.

Pulled him so tight as she planted a kiss on the top of his head.

"I love you."

And with Simon holding her as well, he answered, "Love you too, Mom."

Held for but seconds—then she released him, and turned back to the wall made by the car.

And now, she could also see them coming.

38
Counting Bullets

And now Christie watched them hurrying toward the circle of cars, toward the house, the barn.

A swarm of Can Heads.

Someone off to the right started firing, and again the man on top of the pickup—now their sudden leader—yelled, "Stop. Wait until we can actually see them!" Then, "Save your goddamn ammo!"

She looked at Simon, his handgun pointing out into the darkness, such a terrible sight.

Then she looked back, to the dark line scrambling toward them.

How many are there?

Easily a hundred. Spread out as if each wanted to be the first to reach the people with guns waiting for them.

Eager for that chance to get lucky,

To eat.

Because that's all they did.

The only good thought she had, *Kate wasn't here.*

Though her daughter may be in danger as well, Christie had the sudden thought that even what she was facing could be better than this.

Then, as if talking to him, Christie thought about Jack.

What she would give to have him here.

But then—more importantly—how she needed to be both

mom and dad.

She thought, *I'm a poor substitute, Jack.*

But as soon as she thought that, and continuing that dialogue in her head, she could hear his words, *You have to do the best you can.*

The absolute best.

You can.

She took a breath.

The line of Can Heads, an army of horrors, was closer.

In seconds, everyone would begin firing.

She let the breath out slowly.

*

Driving on the road now seemed so easy. Headlights on. Kids had slowly raised their heads.

And Kate smiled—a quick turn back to them.

"We're okay, you guys. You're safe now."

And did she really believe that? If she knew anything, it was that there was no place that was *really* safe.

But the horror that those kids faced—unimaginable—was over.

And Kate thought, *I helped do that.*

It was an amazing feeling.

And she knew her mom would be so proud. Such a kid thing… wanting a parent to really be proud of them.

But Kate also knew this.

She loved her mother more than anything.

Even Simon too.

That was the important thing to remember. To never let that thought go.

They would be together for as long as possible.

She gave the kids another smile, and rolled along the road, speeding back to the farmhouse, and all the people waiting there.

*

The guns began blasting. The sound erratic.

Rifles, big shotguns, and the lighter firecracker sounds of handguns. Even an automatic rifle using bullets way too fast.

Christie was never more appreciative of the time Jack spent teaching her how to shoot.

She took aim at one figure, pulled the trigger and watched it fall.

She looked over at Simon, so close by, also leaning over the hood of the car, the handgun extended out.

Taking his time.

With every shot, every bullet.

And then, "Got one," he said quietly.

"Good. Nice and slow…"

Both of them, eyes locked on the line now racing toward them.

And Christie felt her fear now twist, start to run into something darker, something overwhelming.

Hopelessness.

Because she could see, with every shot, even if each one was a hit, there were too many of them.

Did they have enough guns, enough bullets to stop them, even with every shot hitting?

And Christie knew the answer to that.

Even as she kept firing—and soon time to reload—she started to think about possibilities.

Thinking that, even with Kate not back, with all those other people with their weapons that could possibly turn the tide, maybe she… and Simon had to escape.

And with each pull of the trigger, her focus scattered between shooting the Can Heads and thinking what to do.

God, what to do?

*

Kate saw the car with the other children right behind them, then in the distance—their headlights pin pricks, like stars that had fallen down to the road—more cars.

Must be the others coming back, she thought.

Though, as she chewed at her lip, there was another possibility.

Unless they lost that battle.

But she shook her head.

Couldn't have happened.

It has to be them.

Then, from the darkness in the back, a voice. So quiet, the words barely audible above the sound of the engines.

"Where..." a girl's voice asked. Then, as the girl cleared her throat, "Where are we going?"

Kate nodded, and then to the mirror to see which one had asked the question.

Someone's eyes locked on hers in the mirror. The girl... a bit taller than the rest.

"Someplace safe," Kate said. "My mom is there, my brother. Other people."

Then a smile.

"You'll be safe there."

*

"Mom, they're running faster," Simon said.

Christie had finished reloading, fumbling in the dark.

She saw that what Simon said was true. As some Can Heads neared their prize, they ran even faster.

Which had the effect of making their advancing line turn into an erratic jumble that made them harder to hit.

She also thought of the one, terrible idea she had.

A possibility.

She, and Simon, could get into the car.

Break the circle, and drive the hell out of here.

But then...

Then, what of Kate? And the circle, suddenly with an opening putting everyone at jeopardy.

But just as she had that desperate thought of escape, she looked to her left.

A car came to life.

Headlights on.

Someone leaving.

The car roared out of the circle, and began to race to the left, to the dirt driveway that led from the farm down to the main road.

But...

Christie could see that the driveway would take the car close to a bunch of Can Heads clustered to the side.

Who had taken notice of the car.

And now with the Can Heads closer, she could see that many of them had rocks in their hands.

The car—which had just created this great opening in the circle, with everyone's eyes both on the attacking Can Heads and the fleeing car—swerved close to that group.

And the Can Heads jumped in the car's path.

Then, the sound of breaking glass as the moving car became covered with Can Heads, like ants all over a piece of sticky food dropped at a picnic.

So fast.

And while it was too dark to really see, Christie watched the car jerk left and right as if whoever was steering it no longer was.

And then it flipped over, stopped.

She heard—even over the sound of the guns firing—screams.

She turned to Simon, who had been watching as well.

"Simon. Out there! Look out *there*. Keep shooting!"

She looked at her son in the dark.

He wasn't crying.

But even with the gun braced on the hood of the car, she saw him shaking.

And she had only one thought then: *We can't have come this far, to have it all end like this.*

We.

Can't.

39
Family

And then Kate, hands locked on the wheel, feeling so strong and good about what happened, could look ahead and see the mayhem.

The flashes of gunfire like fireflies in the summer night.

The gun sounds—some loud, others more like balloon popping—all blending together.

She had just said to the kids in her car, those kids who had been through so much, that they'd be safe.

And now she knew...

That wasn't true.

Then—thinking beyond those kids rattling around in the back as she hit the gas, picking up speed—Kate thought of her mom. Her brother.

So much had fallen on her shoulders lately, Kate knew.

Now this.

The scene before her eyes... terrible.

She kept the accelerator floored as she raced to the circle with its rings of exploding gunfire lights in the night.

And closer to what surrounded that circle.

*

Christie dug into a pocket and pulled out her last shells.

Six of them, quickly sliding them into the gun.

There were so many targets, that even taking her time, even with so many shots, with the Can Heads dropping yards away from her, there was no way she could "slow down."

No way she could conserve bullets.

Simon had done well, and he had more shells, more ammo.

But he also had to be only minutes away from being out as well.

If only the others would get back.

More guns.

They could turn the tide.

Then, without really a look, out of the corner of her eye she saw headlights in the distance.

She took a breath.

They'd be here soon.

But then she heard—amid what was definitely a lessening of gunfire—more screams, the yells.

No need to look.

She knew what that meant.

Then, as if signaling what would happen next, the old woman, mere feet away, said, "I'm out. Last shot. Nothing else, I'm afraid."

And Christie pulled the trigger, shooting with her gun barrel against the head of a Can Head woman—a tattered dress, blood spattered as if crazy makeup—the Can Head collapsed from the blast.

Right at her feet.

Christie said, still targeting the horde, with five... then four... shells left, "The others... they're coming back. They'll be here soon. Just hang on."

Then, crawling over the body of the Can Head that Christie just shot—three, four of them.

Crawling over that body.

Making idle snatches at that Can Head body, stuffing chunks into their mouths as they scrambled toward the car.

There was nothing else to do now.

Even with a few more shots left.

"Simon, start to back away. Get to the house."

He didn't move. So resolute in his job of aiming and slowly pulling the trigger on what was now his overwhelmed handgun.

She yelled, "Simon!"

And then the boy backed up, his eyes locked on the Can Heads reaching the car, suddenly moving even faster with their prey nearby, leaping onto the hood, the roof of the car.

Anna had turned to run as well.

And even as Christie took Simon's hand, she saw Anna take a step away and then get yanked back, like a puppet.

Yanked back. Then disappearing into the sea of Can Heads.

She started, as best she could, to run—the act so painful.

Tugging Simon, who kept looking over his shoulder.

He can run faster than me, Christie knew.

He could get to the house.

But not if he stays with me.

First, she let go of his hand.

Then, over the screams that surrounded them, "Go Simon. Fast as you can. Run."

But he didn't move from her side as she hobbled at what was her top speed.

Then, born of terrible fear, horror, she did something she never had done before.

She slapped her son.

"Run!"

And then, with only the slightest hesitation, his eyes watering now.

Crying now.

He did as he was told.

He started turning.

Which is when Christie felt the first hand grab her.

*

Kate saw an opening in the circle. She plowed the car right into it, sending the bodies of Can Heads flying left and right.

The circle had meant to protect them.

But now there were Can Heads all around it. On the cars, inside the circle itself, people running from them.

In the rearview mirror, she saw the rest of the cars finally getting here.

The people who had attacked the farm, returning to *this*.

Kate drove wildly through the mass of figures in the circle.

Taking care not to hit any fleeing people, and then nudging the car left and right whenever she could take out a Can Head.

The kids in the car screamed constantly now.

But Kate blocked that out. Had to.

She then drove headlong toward the house, nearly right into it as she hit the brake and turned the steering wheel.

She felt the car rock to the right.

The left wheels leaving the ground for a moment before the car was stopped, in a cloud of smoky dry dirt.

She got out, racing as fast as she could. Opening the car doors on the right side.

"Come on. Everyone into the house. *Hurry!*"

The screaming, crying kids didn't move.

Then, because she felt they would know what she was about to say... that she would understand it, "If you want to live, get out of the car."

The older girl sitting in the back finally added her voice to Kate's, with urges of "Come on" and "Hurry."

And not even waiting for the car to empty, for the kids to file into the house, Kate ran in the other direction.

Out to the circle. Where there was still gunfire.

Still people struggling to get back.

Where still—Kate was sure—she'd find her mother, her brother.

*

The hand, feeling like a claw, yanked Christie back.

The pull so strong it forced air out of her lungs.

Then worse, another hand on her.

But, despite being stopped herself, with her eyes looking ahead, she saw Simon.

And despite how fast he ran, a Can Head had grabbed him too, stopped him. She could see the shadowy shape of Simon flailing with his gun, trying to beat the thing away.

But it had to be near twice his height.

And Christie—though held—could still raise her gun.

Not to shoot at the two things that held her, struggling to throw *her* to the ground—but at the one holding Simon.

Her rifle wobbly with all her flailing.

She forced herself not to cry.

Because however could she see? How could she aim if her eyes became teary?

She fired once.

Nothing.

One bullet left.

The gun held at a ridiculous angle, and she was guessing at its aim.

Pulled the trigger.

And then the Can Head staggered back.

Simon was free.

And as if that mission—saving her son—had sapped her of the superhuman strength she had somehow summoned to stay standing, to protect her son… she was quickly thrown to the ground hard.

Slammed into the ground.

Then, she was covered.

They were all over her.

*

Kate raced, her gun out front.

She only fired if a charging Can Head threatened her mad rush past the humans fighting in small groups, still in the circle.

Soon the others would swarm in, the people who had been away with her. Sam, Ben… all the others.

Soon.

Just have to hang on, she thought.

Then she saw Simon.

A quick hand to his face.

"Okay?"

Fast. Just the one word.

A nod.

Then he said, pointing, "Mom!"

"Go," Kate said, not even waiting to see if Simon obeyed.

She began running in the direction of where Simon pointed.

*

Kate could see what was happening here, in the dark—morning light still hours away.

Some people lay on the ground, with other shapes—Can Heads—on top of them, pulling, yanking…

Absorbed.

Others who had come back with her were trying to get those still alive to hurry to the house, while all around clusters of firefights broke out.

The confusion: near total.

She ran full out to where Simon had pointed.

And she saw her mother.

Two of them had her tight and were dragging her to the ground.

Kate ran up and placed her gun against the head of one and pulled the trigger, not caring how it exploded, how the blood flew everywhere.

But then quickly… moving to the other, and doing the same thing.

Then Kate herself felt a yank, dragged quickly backward, the gun nearly flying from her hands as she was thrown to the ground.

And now she shot again, and again, not able to really aim, other than awkwardly, up at the things on her.

Until she heard a man's voice.

Then felt something lifted from her.

A blast.

Then Kate was able to roll free.

And with a bunch of blasts accompanying her moves, with her muttering the word...

"Mom."

She scrambled to stand up.

The gun blasts suddenly stopping. Because it was over.

And standing up, everything so dark, the people shouting, the moans of other people on the ground.

She looked ahead.

Steps away.

Her mother on the ground.

Eyes open.

Alive.

Kate raced to her, falling to her knees.

She saw Sam—who had just saved her—come beside her, yelling at people.

Because...

Kate could look down and she saw—in her mother's midsection—this great hole.

One look.

That's all Kate could handle.

She leaned close, people racing here to help.

Close to her mother's lips.

"Mom, you're going to be..."

It's what they always say.

But the last word was cut off by her mother's lips moving, barely a sound.

But words, right in her ear.

"I love you."

"Mom…"

"So proud."

"Mom, here they are. They'll carry you in."

Her ear still glued to her mother's lips as men—just dark shapes really—leaned down to pick her up.

Yes! And get her inside. Get her medicine, bandages, and…

But her ear, still listening, the words so faint.

"Take care of Simon. Take care—"

Then as she was raised, as Kate, kneeling, leaned back, two—now three—men gently raising her mother up.

The eyes that had seen Kate.

Now looking at nothing. Just a glisten in the darkness.

Staring forever.

And Kate felt a hand on her shoulder as she started shaking her head.

Shaking, and saying, "No."

Then again, each time the word louder, until she just knelt there in the blood-spattered dirt, sobbing, saying the word over and over again.

"No. No. No!"

Until it was a howl, and she didn't care how loud.

The man's hand stayed on her shoulder.

And it would stay there until, finally, Kate had no more energy to cry.

No more energy to howl out that word.

Until… the sky somewhere started to shift from black to purple to a hint of other colors that started appearing.

The night had ended.

And Kate had to keep telling herself over and over again.

The impossible truth.

Unacceptable.

My mom is gone.

There's just me. And Simon.

Just us.

epilogue

40

Bald Mountain, Michigan—Mid-October

Kate waited for the gate to open, and then she started the rocky drive up the slope.

Her partner—people worked in teams here, for a lot of reasons—was a nineteen-year-old boy, sitting beside her, older.

But Kate was the leader.

There had never been any question about that.

The Rav-4 bumped and rattled until they reached a plateau on the hill.

From here, she saw people working out on the terraced fields, some with carts, as they gathered the vegetables that had been grown and—amazingly enough—flourished here.

And down one slope, a stand of apple trees, young; but they too had produced a variety of apples. Many even had the marks of an insect here and there.

No one complained about that.

Somehow, insects coming back.

That meant something.

No one wished these were like the fruits and vegetables that had been modified to resist bugs—only to disappear, succumbing to whatever wiped out crops worldwide.

She pulled the car to a jerky stop beside a line of vehicles.

Sam Lewis stood talking to a man with a great baldhead and giant hands, "Big Jose" they called him, the man who somehow kept all their vehicles running.

"Quite the stop, Kate. You sure you don't want me to drive?"

She turned to Tim sitting beside her.

Though he often kidded her about her decisions when they went out on patrol—about driving, about anything—it all seemed gentle.

So yeah. She liked him.

And he seemed to know it.

"Got us here, didn't I?" she said, popping open the door and getting out.

But not before giving Tim a smile.

She took her rifle out with her. Probably no shooting today, but her gun was never far from her.

Sam saw her and gave her a wave.

With a nod to Tim, she walked over.

"Quiet again?" Sam asked.

"Yes. Saw nothing."

"Okay. What's this? A week straight?"

"Easily. And the other patrols?"

"Same thing."

She saw Sam looked away, to the top of the hill where the brilliant fall sun was about to slip behind it, throwing the valley into deep, cool shade.

"Sam, what do you think it means?" Kate asked.

He turned to her. "Not sure, Kate. But I can tell you what I *hope* it means."

She stood there.

Since her mother died, she noticed that Sam talked to her as an adult. As if whatever Christie had meant, who she was, was now part of Kate.

And in doing that, Sam had helped her during those first terrible weeks without her.

Though she and Simon spent weeks just doing nothing, it was Sam—when they had reached Michigan—who came and said, "We could use you, Kate. And your brother. Lots to be done."

That was it.

Lots to be done.

And if this was their future, their life now—and for who knew how many years ahead—she then realized it was time, in another way, *to move on.*

To somehow let go of that pain.

Knowing one very key thing: It's what her mother would have wanted.

"And what is that... what you hope?" Kate asked.

"Somehow, they're disappearing. Can Heads. Dying off. Turning on each other? Or who knows? Leaving the people here, dunno, safe?"

She watched Sam look around at the valley, at the rows of corn still to be cut down.

Corn.

Again—*amazing.*

Somehow they had been able to get strains that did just fine here.

And not only that, but squash. Even pumpkins! And while dairy and meat were still very scarce, even those few animals they had seemed to be doing okay, with enough water and feed.

Kate knew from meetings they had—where she attended as a full partner—that they now knew there were dozens, maybe hundreds of communities like this scattered throughout the country.

Led by scientists and old-school farmers who together figured out what to grow and what not to... how to naturally and carefully nurture strains of crops that had no connection to whatever mutation made the world's food supply suddenly so vulnerable.

"You really think so?"

Sam looked at her, the still-warm sun on her face, feeling so good.

He smiled. "I said, 'hope.' Can't be sure. And don't worry, you won't be out of a job. Not for some months to come. But if this keeps up... through the winter, into spring... think we'll need to find another job for you other than running around looking for Can Heads."

She laughed at that. "Yeah, could get boring."

"Maybe teach you some science? Maybe you'd like that?"

Kate now looked away.

It was so weird, to stand here, talking of a future.

Making plans.

When not all that long ago, the idea of making plans seemed ridiculous.

"I think I'd like that. I mean, if I'm smart enough."

Sam laughed. "You are. Don't worry about that. Maybe get you working with the hydroponic teams. We're doing well now... but we need to *keep* doing well."

"Until someday, things are normal again, hmm?"

"Normal?"

He laughed. "Yeah."

Sam turned back to the hill. The sun slowly setting. A ritual: sunset, something to be noted.

Another day here.

Another day when things were better.

"Or let's say... closer to normal. Yeah, that's the goal."

Kate took a breath. "Simon still over at the gardens?"

Sam nodded. "Saw him a while ago. He's got the touch, too, you know. Smart kid. Been teaching Ben things as well." He took a breath. "Good, smart kid."

Another nod. "I'm going to go over. Check up on him."

Funny after all these months, Kate still felt the need to "check up."

Make sure her brother was there, was safe.

Her promise to her mother.

"Sure. See you later," Sam said as she walked the rocky trail that led to the eastern slope of the hill, past the row of buildings where plants could be started, sprouts formed, tested… and finally moved to a valuable space on the terraced fields in spring.

Kate waited for the gate to open, then started the rocky drive up the hill.

Matthew Costello
www.mattcostello.com

Matt Costello's award-winning work, across all media, has meshed story, gameplay and technology.

He has written and designed dozens of award-winning and best-selling games including *The 7th Guest*, *G-Force*, *Just Cause* and *Pirates of the Caribbean*. Time Magazine said of *Doom 3*, which he scripted, "The story is delivered with unusual art." *Rage*, which Matt also wrote, won the most Game Critics Awards at E3, including 'Best Console Game'. He continues to write and help create ground-breaking projects games world-wide.

His novels, spanning horror, suspense and mystery, have been published all around the world. His classic horror novel *Beneath Still Waters* was filmed by Lionsgate. His post-apocalyptic novel, *Vacation*, was a major release from St. Martin's Press and is being developed as a film. St. Martin's/Macmillan also released the sequel, *Home* as well as his SF epic novel, *Star Road*.

His short story, "The Last Vanish"—featured in the just-released 13Thirty books anthology, *Uncharted Worlds*—was filmed by Tripp Avenue Productions and has been featured in over a dozen film festivals and is a finalist in the Dramatic Short Category at the Central Florida Film Festival. His mystery series, Cherringham, co-authored with Neil Richards, has sold over 250,000 copies.

Matt has also written episodes and created TV formats for PBS, Disney, SyFy, and the BBC. He consults on story, games and multiplatform projects around the world, and has also created interactive installations for The British Museum, The Brooklyn Museum, Disney and Buckingham Palace. He is currently helping write and design an hour-long VR Experience tied to a very major film release in 2017... about which he cannot say anything... yet.

Other books from 13Thirty Books

~~Never~~ Fear Series:
~~Never~~ Fear
~~Never~~ Fear – Phobias
~~Never~~ Fear – Christmas Terrors
~~Never~~ Fear – The Tarot
~~Never~~ Fear – The Apocalypse

Lights End – Mathew Kaufman
More Than Magick – Rick Taubold

The Third Hour – Richard Devin
Punctuation: Period! for Fiction Writers – Rick Taubold

Heather Graham's Christmas Treasures
Heather Graham's Haunted Treasures

On Two Fronts – Lance Taubold (with Sgt. Adam Fenner)
Ripper A Love Story – Lance Taubold (with Richard Devin)

Pine River Library
395 Bayfield Center Dr.
P.O. Box 227
Bayfield, CO 81122
(970) 884-2222
www.prlibrary.org

CPSIA information can be obtained
at www.ICGtesting.com
Printed in the USA
LVOW13s1813280218
568199LV00016B/1151/P